SARAH DILLARD'S RIDE

BY

JAMES OTIS

CHAPTER I.

A BRITISHER'S THREAT.

In the year there was in North Carolina, west of Broad River, and near the site of what is now known as Rutherfordton, a settlement called Gilbert Town.

Within five or six miles of this village on a certain September day in the year above mentioned, two lads, equipped for a hunting trip, had halted in the woods.

One was Nathan Shelby, a boy sixteen years of age, and nephew of that Isaac Shelby whose name is so prominent in the early history of North Carolina; the other, Evan McDowells, son of Colonel Charles McDowells, was one year younger than Nathan.

But for the fact that these two lads were sorely needed at their homes, both would have been enrolled either among the American forces, or with those hardy pioneers who were then known as Mountain Men, for the time was come when the struggling colonists required every arm that could raise a musket.

On the previous month the American forces under General Gates had been defeated by Cornwallis at Camden. Tarleton had dispersed Sumter's forces at Rocky Mount, and the southern colonists appeared to have been entirely subdued by the royal troops.

General Cornwallis, now at Camden, was bending his efforts to establish the king's government in South Carolina, and in punishing those "rebels" who, despite their many reverses, were yet among the mountains awaiting a favorable opportunity to strike another blow in behalf of freedom.

It was at this time, and especially in the Carolinas, as if the attempt to free the colonists from the oppressive yoke of the British had utterly failed, and even the most sanguine despaired of being able to accomplish anything in that section until General Washington should lend them some assistance.

Nathan and Evan, lads though they were, understood full well the situation of affairs, and as they sat upon the trunk of a fallen tree, resting from the labor of seeking food—for this hunting trip had been made for serious purposes, rather than in pursuit of sport—the two spoke concerning the reverses which had been visited upon the patriots.

"It is as if we were already whipped into submission," Evan said sadly, "for how is it possible our people shall gather in such force as to be able to offer successful resistance?"

"That seems indeed true," Nathan replied, "and yet will Colonel William Campbell of Virginia remain idle? Do you believe my uncle, Colonel Shelby, or Lieutenant-Colonel John Sevier, have laid down their arms? Or even if those three are subdued, is it likely, think you, that your father will rest content while the king's forces overrun the country at their pleasure?"

"There are matters which cannot be mended, however brave men may be, and it seems to me that now has come the time when we must say that the struggle for liberty can no longer be continued."

"If all who have for four years opposed the king's will were as faint-hearted as you, Evan, then indeed had the rebellion been crushed before it was well begun."

"But tell me, Nathan, how may the Americans, with but few men, scanty equipments, and little or no money, even attempt to hold their own against the royal forces, which outnumber us mayhap ten to one?"

"That I cannot do, and perchance even your father might find it difficult to make reply to such question, but this much I believe to be a certainty. The desire for freedom has not been crushed out from the hearts of the American people, and while it remains strong as at present, some way will be found whereby we shall have at least the semblance of an army again."

"I would I could believe you."

"Is your mother thus despondent?"

"I cannot say, Nathan. It is now near two weeks, as you know, since I have seen her."

"But think you she has lost all hope? She, who has dared to burn charcoal in the fireplace of her own home, while the Britishers were about, in order to carry it to your father, who was making gunpowder in a cave among the mountains."

"My mother is brave, which is more, mayhap, than can be said for her son."

"Ay; had she not been, when your father's cattle were driven off by the British skirmishers, she had hardly called the neighbors together, and by such show of strength recovered the property. With women like your mother, and men such as your father and my Uncle Isaac, I tell you, Evan, the cause of liberty is not lost."

"But it would seem as if we were further from our purpose now than four years ago, when a declaration of our independence was read throughout the colonies. Then we had more money, and it was not as difficult to find recruits. Now ten dollars in paper is hardly worth two cents—in fact, I am told that even the troops consider it too cumbersome for its value to repay them for carrying it around."

"That is the case only with the paper money."

"Ay, Nathan; and as for gold and silver, we still trust to that on which is stamped the king's image. But it is not for you and I to talk of political matters, when both are really in the same way of thinking; the only difference between us is that I, who was never so courageous as you, have grown faint-hearted."

Evan ceased speaking very suddenly, for at that instant both the lads heard the hoof-beats of horses in the distance, and started up in what was very like alarm as they listened, while exchanging inquiring glances.

"It must be that the British are coming this way," Evan said, turning as if to flee; but his companion clutched him by the arm, saying with a laugh:

"You are grown timorous indeed, Evan, if you can imagine that noise to be caused by the redcoats. Surely there are none nearabout here, and even though there were, it is not likely they would attempt to make their way through this wood."

Evan ceased his efforts to flee, but turned as if unwilling, with a forced smile upon his face.

"Of course it must be as you say, Nathan, for the Britishers would have no business here; yet it is even true they may be nearabout, for we have heard that General Cornwallis was bent on sending a force into this section, and he is not wise who refuses to take heed of any warning in these times."

"You need not set me down as one who makes light of the information which has been brought by those whom we could trust; but I refuse to be alarmed without cause, and the idea that the Britishers would ride into this thicket is— They are redcoats! It is I who am playing the fool by setting myself up as an authority on those matters of which I know nothing!"

The foremost of a mounted band had come into view, causing this sudden change in Nathan's speech, and the two boys gazed in alarm at the rapidly advancing horsemen, for now was it too late to make any attempt at flight. Both knew, from reports which had been spread through the country, of outrages committed among even those who were not in arms, what it might mean to fall into the hands of the enemy, who were bent on subjugating the country by any means, however harsh, and they had good reason to expect brutal treatment once they were caught in the clutches of the king's troops.

Involuntarily the lads clasped hands. Although armed, there was no thought in the mind of either that resistance might be offered, and indeed it would have been in the highest degree foolhardy to have done other than they did at this moment—quietly await that foe from which escape was impossible.

Where they stood the forest was open and free from underbrush, therefore while the troopers were yet a quarter of a mile away they were in full view, their red coats showing in vivid contrast among the green leaves, and before the advance squad were yet arrived at where the boys were standing, the entire company could be seen.

Fully two hundred men, a goodly portion of whom were Tories, clad in the ordinary garb of the country, and the remainder wearing the king's uniform, made up the party.

Among the foremost of the riders was one clad in the habiliments of a major, and from what had been told by those who brought the information of General Cornwallis' movements, the boys knew at once that this must be Patrick Ferguson of the Seventy-first Royal Regiment.

It was this officer who accosted the frightened lads, by asking in a loud voice which had in it much of menace:

"What are you two doing here armed? Rebel spawn no doubt, who lie in wait to do mischief when it may be accomplished without danger to yourselves."

"We are out hunting, and if it please you, sir, in order to get meat for the family," Nathan replied, speaking stoutly, although he was inwardly quaking with fear.

"Tell me no lies or it shall go the worse with you. How long has it been that you of the Carolinas must search for food in the forests?"

"Since his majesty's troops overrode the colony, quartering themselves upon those whose store of provisions was already scanty."

"Be careful how you speak! I am not in a mood to hear insolence from those who rebel against their lawful king," and the major made a threatening gesture, bending from his horse as if he would strike the boys.

Evan stepped back a pace in fear; but Nathan boldly held his ground as he asked bravely:

"Think you, sir, that two lads like us may do the king harm?"

Major Ferguson's face reddened with rage, and motioning for one of the troopers to advance, he said:

"Disarm and bind these insolent cubs who dare bandy words with their betters. They shall talk in a different strain before I am done with them."

"Would you make prisoners of us who are not soldiers?" Nathan asked even as the man seized him by the arm. "Would you carry away from their homes two boys upon whom a family is depending for food?"

"Where are your fathers?" Major Ferguson asked sharply.

"I have none," Nathan replied. "My mother is a widow."

"And yours?" he continued, turning toward Evan.

"Colonel Charles McDowells."

"As rank a rebel as lives in the Carolinas. See that you bind them well, my man, for I doubt not these two, innocent as they would appear, have already had their fingers in the rebel broth."

"Since you are bent on making us prisoners, sir, it is useless to deny that we have done aught against the king, save it be a crime to perform our share in feeding those dependent upon us."

"If those who make up the ragamuffin following of Mister Washington could not depend on such as you to provide for the women and children, they might be forced to remain at home where they belong, instead of hatching treason, and I could then, perhaps, clear this portion of the colonies of every male inhabitant who is old enough to be of service in any capacity. Before I have performed my mission you of the Carolinas shall understand what rebellion means, for it is my purpose to teach you a lesson."

Having said this the valiant major turned his horse that he might speak with some of his followers, and the trooper who was bidden to disarm and bind the lads had well-nigh finished with the task.

Nathan and Evan were rudely searched, and with such effect that even their spare flints were taken from them. Their hands were bound behind their backs securely with leathern straps; the fowling pieces and the scanty store of ammunition were taken charge of by one of the troopers, and he who had been detailed to seize them stood as if awaiting orders of his commander.

"Keep up a brave heart, Evan," Nathan whispered courageously. "Do not give yonder redcoated brute the satisfaction of seeing that we are afraid."

"We are likely to be carried very far from home, Nathan, and it may be that much suffering is in store for us."

"Of that there can be little doubt; but no good will come to us by showing the white feather, for of how much weight, think you, tears and prayers be upon such as our captor. It would please him were we to give free rein to our sorrow, and I am not minded he shall have such gratification from me."

"But surely there is no reason why you should anger him by bold speaking—that will not avail us."

"No more than it would if we pleaded for mercy, and there is much satisfaction to be gained by depriving him of the pleasure that would come with the sight of our tears. Hold firm, Evan McDowells, as your father and your mother would do were they in like situation, and mayhap the time will come when this Major Ferguson's grasp will be so far lessened that we shall see a chance of slipping through his fingers."

"I have little hope of any such good fortune," Evan replied, with a long-drawn sigh, and then both the boys fell silent.

The horsemen had dismounted, and it was evident that a prolonged halt would be made.

The major gave no further orders concerning his prisoners, and the trooper stood guard over them four or five paces away, giving no apparent heed to the conversation in which they had been indulging.

During half an hour the situation remained unchanged, and then came into view two hundred or more men on foot, the greater number wearing scarlet uniforms, the remainder being evidently Tories.

At first glance the boys believed this last body of Britishers had come by accident upon the halting-place; but as the men exchanged salutations with the members of the advance party, it could be seen that they all formed one company under the leadership of Major Ferguson, and had been temporarily separated because of the more rapid traveling of the horsemen.

When another half-hour had been spent here the order was given to resume the march, and an officer in the uniform of a captain brought word from the major to the man who was guarding the boys, that he would be relieved from duty, one of the foot-soldiers taking his place.

When the change of guards had been effected, Nathan and Evan were ordered into line midway of the column, and thus hemmed in on every side they were forced to advance, traveling with difficulty, and even pain, because their arms were fettered.

As a rule, the men gave very little attention to these young prisoners, save when one or the other of the boys fell slightly in the rear, and then a blow from the butt of a musket would warn him that he must keep pace with the remainder of the troop or suffer because of inability to do so.

Now that the lads were completely surrounded by foes, no conversation of a private nature was possible, and in silence they marched on, with ample food for unpleasant thoughts.

The only question in the minds of both was as to the destination of this body of Britishers, for there seemed little reason why so many men should penetrate this mountainous portion of the Carolinas, where there was no important stronghold to be captured.

Until five o'clock in the afternoon the troop advanced steadily, and then the foot-soldiers were arrived at a small valley where the horsemen had already apparently halted for the night.

Fires were kindled here and there; some of the soldiers were engaged in cooking, others in caring for the horses, and all so intent upon making themselves comfortable that it was as if the prisoners had been forgotten by everyone save him who was charged with their custody.

When an hour had passed the lads were still standing where they had been halted, and Nathan said with a mirthless laugh:

"It looks as though we might be forced to keep our feet until morning, for so nearly as I can make out food has been served to all save ourselves and our guard."

"I am counting on being relieved before many more moments pass," the soldier said petulantly, for Nathan had spoken so loudly that he could not fail to hear the remark.

"And are we to be starved because we neither wear red coats nor are willing to march shoulder to shoulder with them?"

"It matters not to me what disposition may be made of you, so that I am given an opportunity of getting my rations," the soldier said, and a moment later one of his comrades came up, musket in hand, to relieve him.

To this last guard Nathan repeated his question as to the probability of their being provided with supper, and the soldier replied carelessly:

"I am not the quartermaster of this detachment, and if I was I question whether much time would be spent over such as you."

Then he fell to pacing to and fro, watching his comrades as they lounged around the campfire; but all the while keeping close guard over the two lads, who were so weary from the hunting of the forenoon and the march of the afternoon that it is questionable whether they could have fled even if the opportunity presented itself.

"I had expected to be ill-treated," Nathan said with an assumption of carelessness to his comrade; "but did not count on being starved. It is a pity, since we were to be made prisoners, that this gallant Major Ferguson could not have come up after we had partaken of dinner, for it seems as if many hours had passed since we ate breakfast."

Evan was on the point of making some reply to this mournful remark when from the distance he observed a lad, who, coming directly across the valley, was halted by the sentinels stationed around the encampment.

"Look there!" he said, in a low tone of excitement. "If I mistake not, it is Ephraim Sowers, and what may he be doing here among the redcoats?"

"It is as I have always believed," Nathan cried, forgetting that the man who acted as their guard could hear every word he spoke. "Ephraim is neither more nor less than a Tory, and I venture to say he comes now to give information concerning our friends."

"It is not the first time he has met this detachment of men," Evan added, "See! He speaks now with one of the soldiers as to an old acquaintance."

"Who may say for how long he has acted the spy? When it was told on the day before yesterday that he had gold in his possession, I would not believe it; but now it is plain to be seen that there was truth in the statement, and we can say how he earned it."

This Ephraim Sowers was the son of one who claimed to be "a man of peace;" one who by many a loud word had declared that he believed it a sin to resort to arms, whatever the provocation, and, living a near neighbor to the McDowells, was in a position, if it so pleased him, to give much of valuable information to the enemy. Until this moment, however, there had been no suspicion that he might be tempted to play the part of spy, and his son's arrival at this encampment told the boys as plainly as words could have done how it was General Cornwallis had reliable knowledge concerning that portion of the colony, for he had given good proof that he knew who among the inhabitants favored the king or the "rebels."

Ephraim advanced leisurely, and with the air of one who believes he is expected, until his eyes rested upon the prisoners; then he started suddenly, a flush as of shame came over his face for the instant, and straightening himself defiantly, he walked up with a vindictive smile until he was within half a dozen paces of the two lads.

"I had thought that the sight of a redcoat was so displeasing that it went against your stomachs," he said tauntingly, "and yet I find you hobnobbing with Major Ferguson's men."

"It seems that you know who commands this detachment," Evan said sternly, forgetting all his fears now in the anger he felt that this lad whom he had once trusted should have been all the while a Tory.

"I'll warrant you two know as much."

"Ay; but we are here as prisoners, and you have come as a visitor—one who has seen these men before, to judge from the manner in which you accosted them."

"Well, what does that prove?" Ephraim asked, an evil look coming into his eyes.

"It proves you to be a spy, and when we shall make known what has been seen this night, I am thinking neither you nor your peace-loving father will find the Carolinas a pleasant abiding place."

"And I am thinking that when such rebels as you have the chance to tell what has been seen, the rebellion will have been crushed out, for now that you are here, if my words go for anything, you will not soon be set at liberty."

CHAPTER II.

THE TORY'S PURPOSE.

Until the moment when Ephraim Sowers had revealed his true self by coming into the British camp as a spy, neither Nathan nor Evan had felt any grave anxiety regarding the future.

They knew full well that the redcoats were not given to being friendly in their intercourse with the so-called rebels, and that such persons as they took were treated with roughness, if not absolute harshness.

Such treatment as had previously been dealt out to captured Americans the boys could endure without a murmur, therefore there was no painful anxiety regarding the outcome of the matter; but when Ephraim Sowers appeared, the situation of affairs seemed to be decidedly changed.

Now that he had been recognized by these two, the news that he was a Tory and in league with the Britishers would be carried to all that country roundabout where he lived, whenever Nathan and Evan were set free.

It was only reasonable to suppose he had some slight degree of influence in the camp, having served Major Ferguson as a spy, and these two lads might safely count on his doing whatsoever was in his power to have them held prisoners, even if worse did not follow, and it was evident Nathan feared this last possibility, for he said in a low tone to his comrade, when the young Tory had walked away with a swagger in the direction of Major Ferguson's tent:

"No good will come to us through having seen that villain."

"On such a point there need be little discussion, for I am of the same mind, and it will be exceedingly fortunate if he leaves this encampment without having worked us some harm, although I cannot say in what way it might be done."

"For his own safety, should he ever count on returning home, we must be silenced, Evan, and I am thinking Ephraim Sowers knows in this encampment enough of his own kidney who would aid him in thus doing."

"Do you mean that he would dare to kill us?" and now Evan looked up in alarm.

"He would dare do anything when there was no danger of his receiving bodily injury. But don't let me play upon your fears, for there is no reason why we should look abroad for trouble when we have sufficient of it close around us. We will trust to the chances that that young Tory is powerless, or too much occupied just at present, to give evil heed to us."

"The last is what we should not take into consideration, for however actively engaged he may be it is necessary for his own safety, should he ever return among his neighbors, to prevent us from telling what we have just learned."

"If you refuse such comfort as I try to give, then we will put it that he will be content so long as we are held prisoners here, and who shall say that we may not soon find an opportunity for escape? Captives while on the march are not like to be kept under overly strict guard."

"Where did the Tory go? I was so bewildered both by seeing him here and realizing what his coming might mean, as to be almost in a daze while he was making his threats."

"I fancied I saw some onenearabout Major Ferguson's tent beckoning for the scoundrel, and he hurried away as if bent on visiting the commander. I venture to predict we shall see him again before he leaves this locality."

Then the lads fell to speculating as to how long young Sowers had been engaged as a British spy; what might be the result of Major Ferguson's march through the mountains, and in other ways discussing the situation as if they were to be spectators rather than participants in whatever might occur.

When half an hour had passed, much to their surprise, for the boys had come to believe they would not be given food that night, rations were served out to them, and they were partaking of the limited meal with such keenness of appetite and eagerness as to be unaware of Ephraim Sowers' return until he stood close beside them.

"Well, have you finished giving Major Ferguson all the information he desired?" Nathan asked curtly, only glancing toward the newcomer sufficiently to discover his identity.

"I may have told him some things that wouldn't be pleasant for you to hear," the Tory replied surlily.

"Of that I have no question, for it is easy to guess that you have done all the injury to your neighbors of which your tongue was capable."

"I have given the major such a good account of you two that he won't be likely to part company with you for some time to come."

"We are not surprised, because it was only what might have been expected after we found you were playing the part of spy," Evan said, determined to so far hide his fears that this vicious enemy should not suspect what was in his heart.

"I am ready to do whatsoever I can against the enemies of the king," Evan replied, assuming what he intended should be a dignified attitude.

"His majesty must rest content now, if he knows that you stand ready to aid his officers by playing the spy upon those who have befriended you when you were in need."

Nathan spoke distinctly and deliberately, in a tone so loud that all might hear, and Ephraim's face crimsoned with mingled rage and shame, for he knew full well that but for the aid afforded him by Nathan's uncle during the previous winter his sufferings might have been great indeed.

"I shall do all in my power to overthrow the wicked plans of the rebels, and more particularly will I exert myself against the Mountain Men," he cried, in a fury of passion, whereat Evan added quietly:

"We can well fancy that, for Master Isaac Shelby is a Mountain Man, and but for him you would have starved. Let me see: vipers have been supposed to be the only living things that would sting the hand which feeds them."

"I shall sting you even worse than I have already done!" Ephraim cried, shaking his clinched hand in impotent rage, and so threatening was his attitude that the soldier on guard seized him, as if fearing the boy would strike the helpless prisoners.

"Take your hands off!" Ephraim cried, literally trembling with passion. "I am not to be treated as a prisoner in this camp after all I have done."

"Very true," the soldier replied quietly. "You shall not be deprived of your liberty save when it becomes necessary to prevent you from striking helpless captives, and that I would not allow my own comrade to do."

"I had no idea of touching them."

"Your actions told a different story, and even though these two lads be rebels, they shall be treated decently while I am on guard over them."

"I will see them hanged, and that before long!" Ephraim screamed.

The soldier released his hold of the infuriated Tory, but took the precaution of stepping directly in front of Nathan and Evan, as if to afford protection; while Ephraim, standing a few paces away, poured out a flood of invective, during the course of which much information was gained by those whom he menaced.

"I didn't come to this place empty-handed!" he cried, "nor will my visit be of little concern to the rebels! I brought Major Ferguson information that Clarke and his men are in camp at Greene's Spring, and to kill and capture them all will be a simple matter for this troop."

"You have dared bring the enemy down upon your mother's own cousin," Evan cried in astonishment.

"He is no cousin of mine once he raises his hand against the king."

"I'll venture to say there will be little desire on his part to claim relationship after he knows the part you have been playing," Nathan replied with a laugh, which yet further increased the Tory's wrath. "But have a care, Ephraim Sowers. The men in this colony are not easily whipped into submission, nor do they readily forget an enemy, and if it should so chance, as it has many times since '76, that the king's forces were driven out of the Carolinas, your life would not be an enviable one."

"If anything of that kind should happen, and I am ready to wager all I possess it never will, you won't be here to know what comes to me, for before then I will take good care you are put where all rebels should be—under the sod."

"If the king's officers will commit, or permit, murder at your request, then must they give up all claim to the name of soldiers," and now Evan was rapidly becoming as excited as the Tory. "It may be you can succeed in having us killed; but the reckoning will come, Ephraim Sowers, and the longer it is deferred the more must you pay."

"I will settle with you first after my own fashion, and when that has been done we will see what your ragamuffin friends are able to do about it."

Ephraim would doubtless have indulged in further threats, but just at that instant a soldier came up from the direction of Major Ferguson's tent, and the vindictive lad was summoned to the commander's quarters.

"It seems that his footing here is not so secure that he can give his tongue free rein many minutes at a time," Nathan said in a tone of relief as the spy walked reluctantly away, literally forced so to do by the messenger who had come in search of him.

"It is not his words which trouble me," Evan said mournfully. "Just now he is in a position to work us great injury, and by yet further provoking his wrath we have made of him even a more bitter enemy than he naturally was."

"I question if that could be possible."

"Yet you cannot dispute his power to work us harm."

"Neither do I. If he be willing, as it appears he has shown himself, to betray the whereabouts of Colonel Clarke's forces, knowing full well that this troop can readily cut them down, it is certain we stand a good show of learning how great is his power for mischief."

"For myself I have little concern at this moment, because of the knowledge that our friends are in such peril."

"And yet there is nothing we can do to aid them."

"Unless it might be we could escape." Evan said suddenly, lowering his voice to a whisper lest the sentinel should overhear his words.

"It is only needed that you look about in order to see how much hope there is of such a possibility," Nathan said despondently. "Even though we were fresh, instead of so weary that I question if we could travel a single mile further, and if we might so far elude the sentinel as to gain the cover of the thicket, it would be impossible to continue the flight two miles, for the Tories in this troop know the country as well, if not better, than we."

"I was not so foolish as to believe that escape might be possible, but only spoke because my thoughts were with those who are threatened, and my desire is to aid them."

"I wish it might be done," Nathan replied with a long-drawn sigh, and then the two fell silent, each occupied with his own gloomy thoughts.

An hour passed, and nothing more had been seen or heard of the Tory spy.

Even though they were in such desperate straits, the boys began unconsciously to yield themselves up to slumber, and after a time, bound as they were, both were reclining upon the green turf in at least partial repose.

When morning came they ached in every limb, with arms so benumbed that it was as if those useful members had been paralyzed. They had slept fitfully, and were hardly more refreshed than when the halt was called after the day's march.

Scanty rations were served out to them, and to the intense relief of both the lads a captain, more humane that his commander, ordered that the bonds be taken from their arms.

They were to be tied together in such manner that any attempt at flight would be useless, and yet the labor of marching would be much lightened.

The prisoners had expected another visit from the Tory before the troop started; but in this they were happily disappointed, and when the march was begun they almost believed Ephraim Sowers had been left behind, until shortly before noon they saw him riding with the mounted detachment.

"He is most likely guiding the force to Greene's Spring," Nathan said bitterly. "He counts on seeing those who have played the part of friends to him shot down, and even though their blood will be upon his head, he is well pleased."

To the relief of both the boys, their enemy did not come near where they were, and it was reasonable to suppose Major Ferguson, although not prone to be overcareful of the feelings of his "rebel" prisoners, had given Sowers orders to put a check upon his tongue.

When noon came the detachment of foot soldiers arrived at Martin Drake's plantation, where the cavalry had already halted and were actively engaged in wantonly destroying property.

Outbuildings were torn down, lambs, chickens, and geese were being slaughtered although they were not needed for food, and the household furniture which, rude though it was, represented all that went to make up the interior of the home, was thrown about the grounds, or chopped into kindlings, from sheer desire to work destruction.

The horsemen could not have been at this place more than an hour when the foot soldiers came up, and yet in that short time they had completely wrecked the dwelling portion of the plantation, and caused such a scene of devastation as would lead one almost to believe that a desperate conflict had raged at that point.

"All this must be pleasing to Ephraim Sowers," Evan said bitterly, "for it was Martin Drake's wife who tended him when he was ill with the fever, and this may be a satisfactory way of requiting her."

"Have you seen him since we halted?"

"No, and I am hoping he has gone ahead with the advanced detachment, for it seems certain all of the horsemen are not here."

Although Master Blake's live stock had been slaughtered in such quantities that there was treble the amount of food the troop could consume, the boys were given nothing more than cornbread for dinner, and hardly so much of that as would suffice to satisfy their hunger.

Not until everything portable had been destroyed, the doors torn from the house, and the windows shattered, was the march resumed, and then the prisoners heard the Tory who was acting as guide say that at nightfall they would camp on Captain Dillard's plantation.

There was in this information a ray of hope, so far as warning Colonel Clarke's men of what threatened, for Captain Dillard was in his command, and if information could be conveyed to the mistress of the house it was possible she might send a message ahead.

This much in substance Nathan had suggested to his comrade; but Evan failed to see any possibility that good might be effected so far as the friends of the cause were concerned.

"Even though Mrs. Sarah Dillard can be told all that we know, it is not likely she will have an opportunity of sending a messenger from the plantation. Ephraim Sowers knows full well where the captain may be found, and will warn Major Ferguson against permitting any person to leave the place."

"If Dicey Langston, a girl only sixteen years old, could baffle Cunningham's band, who gave themselves the name of the Bloody Scouts, as she did on that night when alone she crossed the Ennoree, swollen though the waters were, what may Sarah Dillard do when she knows her husband's life hangs in the balance?"

"It is not a question of what she would do, but of what she can," Evan replied gloomily. "Thanks to Ephraim Sowers, the commander of this force will know only too well how eager she must be to send news ahead of his whereabouts, and will take precautions accordingly."

"That is as may be. We can at least hope for the best," Nathan replied bravely, and then word was given for the troop to resume the march.

During the afternoon the British soldiery came upon two plantations, the buildings of which they utterly wrecked, shooting from sheer wantonness the live stock that could not be run down without too much labor, and seeming eager in every way to mark their trail by destruction.

It was an hour before sunset when the boys saw in the distance the buildings of the Dillard plantation, and knew that the time was near at hand when, if ever, they must get word to that little band whose lives were in such deadly peril.

Ephraim Sowers was nowhere to be seen; but slight comfort could be derived from this fact, for it seemed reasonable to suppose he was making himself obnoxious in the dwelling of those people whom he had once claimed as his friends, but was now visiting as their bitterest enemy.

"Keep your wits about you for the first opportunity to gain speech with Sarah Dillard," Nathan whispered to his comrade, and Evan sighed as he nodded in reply, for it seemed to him there was little chance they would be permitted to hold a conversation with any acquaintance, because of the probable fact that Ephraim Sowers would guard against such a proceeding.

The prisoners were marched directly up to the dwelling, and there, with the windows and doors flung wide open, they had a full view of the entire interior, but their enemy was nowhere to be seen.

This, to Evan, unaccountable absence, troubled him not a little, for he believed it betokened yet more mischief on the part of the vindictive Tory, but Nathan was not so ready to take alarm.

"It may be that he is keeping out of sight, hoping Sarah Dillard will still look upon him as a friend, and, in case the captain should succeed in escaping, confide the secret of his whereabouts to him."

The mistress of the house was doing all in her power to satisfy the exacting demands of the officers who had quartered themselves upon her, as the boys could see while they remained halted near the doorway.

It appeared that such servants as she had were not sufficient in numbers to please these fastidious red-coated gentlemen, and they had insisted that Mrs. Dillard should perform her share of waiting upon them. Now one would call out some peremptory order, and then follow it with a demand that the mistress of the house give it her especial attention, while, despite such insolence, Sarah Dillard moved with dignity here or there, as if it were pleasure rather than necessity which caused her to so demean herself.

On the outside roundabout the soldiers were engaged in their customary diversion of killing every animal which came within range of their guns, and a huge bonfire had been built of the corncribs, near which a score or more of men were preparing the evening meal.

A spectator would have said that the dwelling itself was spared only because in it the officers had taken up their quarters, and once they were ready to depart it would be demolished as the other structures surrounding it had been.

During half an hour or more the boys stood close by the door under close guard, and then one of the officers appeared to have suddenly become conscious of their existence, for he called in a loud tone to Mrs. Dillard:

"We desire of you, madam, some apartment which will serve as a prison for two rebel cubs that we have lately taken. Can the cellar be securely fastened?"

"There is only a light lattice-work at the windows, which might readily be broken out if your prisoners made an effort at escape," Mrs. Dillard replied.

"But surely you have some apartment which will answer our purpose? If not, the men can speedily nail bars on the outside of one of the chamber windows."

"There is a room above, the window of which is already barred, that may serve your purpose," Mrs. Dillard said, as she glanced toward the boys with a certain uplifting of the eyes, as if to say that they should not recognize her as an acquaintance.

"Show it to me and we will soon decide if that be what is required, or whether we shall call upon our troopers to turn carpenters," the officer said with a laugh, as if believing he had given words to some witticism, and in silence Mrs. Dillard motioned one of the servants to lead the way to the floor above.

The brief survey which he made appeared to satisfy the Britisher, for on his return he said to Major Ferguson, who was seated at the head of the table, giving his undivided attention to the generous supply of food which the mistress of the house had been forced to bring out:

"There is but one window in the room of which our fair hostess spoke, and that overlooks the stable-yard; it is barred on the outside with oaken rails stout enough to resist the efforts of any three of our troopers, I should say. The door can be not only bolted, but locked on the outside, and in my opinion there should be no need of a sentinel stationed inside the building."

"If such is the case, why spend so much breath in describing the dungeon," Major Ferguson said with a laugh. "It is enough for our purpose if the lads cannot break out, and the sooner they are lodged within the sooner you will be ready to hold your peace, thus giving me an opportunity of enjoying this admirable game pie. Put the rebels away and sit down here, for it may be many days before another such chance presents itself."

Word was passed to the soldier who had the prisoners in charge for him to take them to the upper floor, and this trifling matter having been arranged, the gallant British officers turned their attention once more to converting their hostess into a servant.

CHAPTER III.

A DESPERATE VENTURE.

The meaning look which Mrs. Dillard had bestowed upon the prisoners, brief though it was, sufficed to revive their spirits wonderfully. Not that there was any promise in it; but it showed they were recognized by the hostess and, knowing her as they did, the boys knew that if there was a loophole of escape for them she would point it out.

While preceding the soldier up the stairs it was much as though they were guests in Sarah Dillard's home, and there came with the fancy a certain sense of relief and security such as had not been theirs for many hours.

The apartment selected to serve as prison was by no means dismal; it was cleanly, like unto every other portion of Sarah Dillard's home, and sufficiently large to permit of moderate exercise, with a barred window overlooking the stable-yard which allowed all that took place in the rear of the dwelling to be seen.

"I shouldn't mind being a rebel myself for a few hours in order to get such quarters as these," the soldier said as he followed the boys into the chamber. "Not a bad place in which to spend the night."

"With a couple of blankets a body might be very comfortable," Nathan replied in a cheery tone, for despite the dangers which threatened that little band at Greene's Spring, despite Ephraim Sowers' avowed enmity and probable ability to do harm, despite the fact that he was a prisoner, this enforced visit to Captain Dillard's house was so much like a home-coming that his spirits were raised at once.

"And you have the effrontery to ask for blankets after getting such a prison as makes a soldier's mouth water," the Britisher said with a certain rough good-nature in his tone. "You rebels have a precious queer idea of this sort of business, if you can complain because of lack of blankets."

"I am not complaining," Nathan replied with a laugh. "Of course there is no situation which cannot be bettered in some way, and I was simply speaking of how this might be improved. We are satisfied with it, however, as it is."

"And so you had better be, for I am thinking there are not two rebel prisoners as comfortably bottled up, and by this time to-morrow night you will be wishing yourselves back," replied the guard.

Then the soldier locked and barred the door on the outside, trying it again and again to make certain it could not readily be forced open, and a few seconds later the sound of his footsteps told that the boys were comparatively alone for the time being.

Now was come the moment when they should make known the danger which threatened the friends of freedom through Ephraim Sowers' perfidy, for every second might be precious if a warning message could be sent, and involuntarily both the lads ran to the window, looking eagerly out through the bars in the hope of seeing some member of the household whose attention might be attracted.

Major Ferguson's subordinates were not so careless as to allow their prisoners many opportunities of such a nature. All the servants, and in fact every person on the plantation, was kept busily engaged waiting upon the redcoats, a goodly number of whom could be seen in the stable-yards, which knowledge caused Evan to say mournfully:

"We are not like to get speech with any one who could carry word to Greene's Spring. It stands to reason Ephraim Sowers has warned the Britishers that such an attempt might be made, and you may be certain, Nathan, no one can leave the plantation without Major Ferguson's permission."

"It is possible he can prevent a message being carried; but I shall not give up hope yet awhile."

"Before many hours have passed the troop, or at least a portion of it, will set out to slaughter our friends. I would I knew where that Tory spy was at this moment!"

"Most likely he has gone ahead to make sure his victims do not escape. We shall hear of him again 'twixt now and daybreak."

"I am afraid so," Evan replied with a long-drawn sigh, and then, leaning his forehead against the wooden bars, he gazed out longingly in the direction his feet would have taken had he been at liberty.

With two hours' start he might save the lives, perhaps of a hundred men, all of whom could be accounted his friends, and yet because of one lad's wickedness that little band of patriots was in imminent danger of being massacred.

From the apartments below the coarse laugh and coarser jest of a Britisher could be heard, telling that the enemy were still bent on making themselves as obnoxious to the inmates of the household as was possible, while now and then from the outside came sounds of the splintering of wood or the cackling of poultry as the soldiery continued their work of wanton destruction.

Both officers and men grew more nearly quiet as the shadows of night began to lengthen. The Britishers were weary with asserting their pretended right as victors, and the stable-yard was well-nigh deserted of its redcoated occupants.

The young prisoners were standing near the window in silence, when a slight noise as of some animal scratching at the door attracted their attention, and instantly the same thought came into the mind of each.

Sarah Dillard, freed for the time being from the exacting demands of the unwelcome visitors, had come, perchance, to point out some way of escape.

Now was arrived the moment when they might reveal to this brave woman the dangers which threatened, and yet for the instant Nathan hesitated so to do, because it appeared to him that he would be distressing her needlessly, since it was hardly probable she could find means of conveying the warning to those in peril. By making her acquainted with all that threatened he would be doing no more than to increase her distress of mind.

Evan, however, was not looking so far into the future. He only realized that perhaps now was the moment when he would make known Ephraim Sowers' perfidy, and crept noiselessly toward the door, whispering eagerly:

"Is that you, Mistress Dillard?"

"Yes, boys, and I have come in the almost vain hope that it may be possible to serve you, although I know not how. When did you fall into the hands of the enemy?"

"Have you seen Ephraim Sowers here?" Evan asked, heeding not the question.

"No. Has he also been made prisoner?"

"It is far worse than that. He is a spy in the service of the redcoats, and has revealed to them the whereabouts of Colonel Clarke's band."

"That is impossible, for the entire company were here not more than eight hours ago, and with them was my husband."

"Then the miserable spy is mistaken, and these Britishers will have their journey for their pains," Nathan whispered in a tone of intense relief. "Ephraim has told Major Ferguson that they were encamped at Greene's Spring, and there——"

"And it is to Greene's Spring they are going!" Mrs. Dillard cried unconsciously loud. "How could any spy have learned of their intended movements?"

"You must remember that Ephraim Sowers has not been looked upon as a spy. Perchance no one except the Britishers knew it until we two saw him coming into the camp where we were prisoners," and Nathan spoke hurriedly. "It is not for us to speculate how our friends have been betrayed; but to give the warning to them without loss of time."

Mrs. Dillard did not reply immediately, and the prisoners could well fancy that she was trying to decide how the danger might best be warded off.

"Is it not possible for you to release us?" Nathan asked after a brief pause. "If either Evan or I were at liberty we might be able, by rapid running, to cover the distance between here and Greene's Springs before the redcoats could arrive there, for it is not likely they will start very early in the night."

"To escape from the window while the soldiers are in the stable-yard is impossible," Mrs. Dillard replied, much as though speaking to herself, "and as for getting you out by this way I am powerless. One of the officers has a key to the door, and even if it was in our possession, there is little chance you could make your way through the house secretly."

"But something must be done, and at once," Nathan whispered in an agony of apprehension, and at that moment the sound of footsteps on the floor below caused Mrs. Dillard to beat a retreat.

The boys could hear the swish of her garments as she ran through the hallway, and it was as if the good woman had no more than hidden herself from view before the heavy footsteps of a man on the stairs told that some one of the Britishers was coming to make certain the prisoners were securely confined.

Creeping noiselessly away from the door lest the redcoat should enter and find them in a position which betokened that they had been holding converse with some one on the outside, the lads remained silent and motionless until the noise of footsteps told that this cautious Britisher, having satisfied himself all was as it should be, had returned to the floor below.

Then the lads stole softly back near the door where they awaited the coming of the woman whom they hoped might show them the way to freedom, even though at the time it seemed impossible she could do so.

The moments passed like hours while she remained absent, and then once more they heard a faint scratching at the door which told of her return.

"Tell me all you know regarding this boy Sowers being a spy," Mrs. Dillard whispered when she was once more where private conversation could be carried on, and Nathan said nervously:

"Why speak of him at a time when every moment is precious? Instead of giving such as that villain a place in our thoughts we should be trying to form some plan whereby the lives of our friends may be saved."

"It is yet too early in the night for us to make any move," the brave woman replied as if her mind was already made up to a course of action. "Until the men have quieted down somewhat we cannot so much as cross the yard without being challenged, and I would know all that may be told before setting out for Greene's Spring."

"Do you count on making such a venture?" Evan asked in surprise.

"Some one must do it, and since I cannot set you free, I must act as messenger."

"But there is hardly one chance in a hundred you will succeed."

"Yet I shall try to take advantage of that hundredth chance."

"But how may you get there? It is twenty miles over a rough mountain road."

"Even though it were ten times as far, and the peril greater an hundredfold, do you not think I would brave it in the hope of saving the lives of those brave men?"

Evan ceased to find objections to her plan; but asked how she might be able to make the journey.

"There is in the stable a colt which the Britishers will hardly attempt to drive away because he has not yet been broken. I shall do my best at riding him, and trust in the good God for protection."

Nathan was not a cowardly lad; his acquaintances spoke of him as one having much courage, and yet he trembled at the thought of this woman attempting to bridle an unbroken colt, and then ride him twenty miles over the rough mountain roads where only the steadiest of horses might safely be used.

He would have said something in the hope of dissuading her from her purpose; but it was as if his tongue refused its office, for Sarah Dillard would ride that night not only to save a hundred or more friends of freedom, but to save the life of her husband.

"Tell me all you know of the spy, so that I may warn our people against him with fair proof."

Neither Evan nor Nathan made any attempt at giving advice; the woman's courage so far eclipsed theirs that it was as if she should command and they obey—as if they had no right even to offer a suggestion. Obedient to her wishes they repeated all they had heard the vindictive Tory say, and described in detail his reception at Major Ferguson's camp.

"If you could only take us with you, or what would be better, so manage it that we might go in your stead," Nathan said when his account of Ephraim Sowers was brought to an end.

"I would willingly do so if it might be possible; but I can see no way to accomplish such a purpose."

"Yet there are many chances against your being able to ride the colt, however willing you may be," Evan said, as if hoping such suggestion might cause her to devise another means of forwarding the warning.

"I know full well how many chances there are against success, and yet because it is the only hope, I shall venture."

But little conversation was indulged in after this assertion, which seemed prompted by despair.

Nathan told the brave woman all he knew regarding the most direct path through the thicket to the American encampment, and Evan warned her to be on the alert for Sowers nearabout the spring, where both he and his comrade believed the spy had gone to make certain his intended victims did not escape.

Then all fell silent as if awed by the dangers which were to be voluntarily encountered, and presently the boys knew from the faint sounds that Sarah Dillard had stolen swiftly away without so much as a word of adieu.

"She will never be able to get an unbroken colt out of the stable, even if she succeeds in bridling him," Evan whispered, and Nathan replied with a certain hopefulness in his tone, although he was far from believing the venture might succeed:

"It is possible the task may be accomplished. I have more faith in her gaining the mastery of the colt for a certain time than I have of her being able to keep him on the trail. There are many places 'twixt here and Greene's Spring where a single misstep, such as an untrained animal is likely to make, will send them both into eternity."

As if by a common impulse the boys moved toward the window, and there stood gazing out, waiting for the appearance of the brave woman who had not only to master an untamed horse, but to keep herself concealed from view while surrounded by enemies.

The troopers' steeds had been stabled in the huge barns to the right of the dwelling, where were kept the draft animals, and, as the boys well knew,

Captain Dillard's saddle horses and the colt to which his wife had referred, were housed in the small building directly across the stable-yard from the improvised prison.

This particular portion of the plantation appeared to be entirely abandoned by redcoats; but the officers in the dwelling were so near at hand that any unusual noise in or around the yard would immediately attract their attention, even though the sentinels were remiss in their duty, and it seemed well-nigh impossible that Sarah Dillard could so much as lead the most steady animal out into the open without betraying her movements to the enemy.

"She won't be able to bridle the colt without something of a fight," Evan said half to himself, and Nathan added as if he would find some ray of hope in the gloom which surrounded them:

"It is fortunate that the stable has no floor, and the colt may do considerable prancing around without giving an alarm."

"Yet it is not likely she can ride him out without a certain amount of noise."

"I know the venture is a desperate one," Nathan replied mournfully; "but I am forcing myself to believe it may succeed."

At this instant a dark form was seen moving cautiously around the corner of the house in the direction of the small stable, and the boys knew that the desperate venture was begun.

Although the night had fully come it was not so dark but that surrounding objects could be seen with reasonable distinctness, and from the moment Sarah Dillard thus came in view the prisoners were able to follow her every movement.

No frontiersman could have made his way across the yard with less noise than she did; not so much as the breaking of a twig betrayed her movements, and if this stealing out of the house had been the only difficult part of her task, then one might say she would accomplish it readily.

The boys hardly dared to breathe as she came from the shadows of the building, moving with reasonable rapidity across the yard until she was lost to view in the gloom of the stable, and then, although no creaking of hinges betrayed her purpose, both knew she had effected an entrance.

It was only the easiest portion of the work which had been accomplished, however, and the prisoners stood with every nerve strained to its utmost tension as they listened for what would betoken that the struggle with the untamed animal had begun.

Once, just for an instant, they saw her form at the door, and then she suddenly disappeared as if the colt had pulled her back; but as yet, even though on the alert, they could hear nothing unusual, and unless the British officers grew suspicious because of her absence, she was yet in safety.

One, two, three moments passed almost as if they were hours, and then the brave woman could be seen fondling and petting the colt, who already wore the bridle, as she peered out from the doorway to learn if the coast was yet clear.

"She has bridled him, and without making a noise," Evan whispered in a tone of astonishment.

"It was easier to do that in the darkness than it would have been in the light, and if she is wise she will mount inside, instead of trying to do so out here."

It was as if Nathan had no more than spoken when with a bound the colt, bearing on his back the woman who was risking her life to save her husband, came over the threshold, rearing straight up on his hind feet until there seemed every danger he would topple backward; but yet his rider kept her seat.

"I had never believed a woman could do that," Evan exclaimed in a whisper.

"Perhaps this one might not have been able to but for the necessity. It hardly seems possible she can get out of the yard without detection, for the sound of his hoofs as he rears and plunges must of necessity bring the redcoats out in the belief that their own horses have been stampeded."

The colt struggled desperately to free himself from the strange burden upon his back, and yet, singularly enough, never once did he come down upon the ground with sufficient force to cause alarm. He alternately reared and plunged while one might have counted ten, his rider clinging to him meanwhile as if she had been strapped securely down, and then with a bound he cleared the stack of brush which was piled just behind the stable, disappearing an instant later amid the forest, which on this side the plantation had been left standing within a hundred yards of the dwelling.

"She is off, and headed in the right direction," Nathan said in a tone of amazement, as if it was almost incredible the feat had been accomplished, and the words were no more than uttered before out of the house came trooping half a dozen men, alarmed by the thud of the animal's hoofs.

"They have heard her," Evan cried in an agony of apprehension, "and now the chase will begin, for they must understand what her purpose is in thus running away."

Fortunately for the safety of that little band at Greene's Spring, the Britishers were not so well informed by the noise of all that had taken place as Evan believed.

The thud of the colt's feet had simply caused them to believe there might be a disturbance among their own animals, and they were very far from suspecting the real truth of the matter.

They went hurriedly toward the barns wherein their horses were stabled, however, and seeing this both the boys believed that chase was about to be given.

"If she can keep the colt straight on the course, I have no fear they will overtake her," Nathan said, much as though speaking to himself; "but it is not probable the beast will be so tractable."

Now the prisoners watched in anxious suspense to see the first of the troop ride out in pursuit, and as the moments passed their spirits increased almost to bewilderment because no such move was made.

Finally, one by one, the redcoats returned to the house as if satisfied everything was as it should be, and Evan whispered, as if doubting the truth of his own statement:

"It must be that they fail to suspect anything is wrong. There is yet a possibility, Nathan, that Sarah Dillard will accomplish the task which half an hour ago I would have said was absolutely beyond her powers."

"And if she can bridle and mount the beast, I am tempted to believe she may reach Greene's Spring in time, for certain it is that up to this moment no one suspects that she has left the plantation."

"I could——"

Evan ceased speaking very suddenly, and it was with difficulty he could repress a cry of fear, for at this instant the key was turned in the lock, the door flung open, and as the prisoners suddenly faced around, they saw before them Ephraim Sowers, looking satisfied and triumphant.

CHAPTER IV.

THE STRUGGLE.

The first and most natural thought that came into the minds of the boys, as they turned to see their enemy standing in the doorway, was that he had discovered the flight, and, perhaps, counted on doing something toward checking it even now, when Sarah Dillard must have been a mile or more away.

Almost as soon as this idea presented itself, however, both realized that if the grinning Tory had even so much as a suspicion of the real state of affairs he would be urging the troopers on in pursuit, rather than standing idly there.

The young scoundrel remained for an instant in the doorway enjoying his triumph, and Nathan found it difficult to repress a smile of satisfaction as he saw the spy thus unsuspicious, while Sarah Dillard was speeding toward Greene's Spring to carry the warning which, if told, would most likely save the lives of a hundred men.

Ephraim, firmly convinced that nothing could avert the fate shaped by him for Colonel Clarke and his force, was enjoying the situation as pictured in his mind, to the utmost of his mean nature, and the boys almost forgot they were prisoners in the pleasure born of the knowledge that the Tory might yet be outwitted.

"What are you fellows doing over there by the window?" Ephraim asked peremptorily after surveying the two in silence fully a moment.

"Have the Britishers any law or rule which forbids one deprived of liberty from seeking fresh air whenever he may be so fortunate as to get an opportunity?" Nathan asked sharply.

"Hark you, Nathan Shelby, I am tired of hearing your long-winded speeches, and we will have done with them from this out—at least, so long as I am the master."

"So long as you are the master!" Evan repeated in a tone of contempt. "We haven't been aware that such was the case."

"Then you may know it now for a certainty. I am counting on you two trying to escape, and therefore have come to stand guard in this room."

"And a valiant guard you will be, Ephraim Sowers, if your courage is no greater than it was one year ago, when you fled in hot haste from what proved to be a turkey-cock, thinking you saw the head of an Indian among the weeds," Nathan said jeeringly, and the spy retorted angrily:

"Have a care over your tongue, my bold rebel! Matters have changed now from what they were forty-eight hours ago. You are among those who obey the king, and do not allow sedition-breeders free rein of their tongues."

"And now hark you, Master Sowers," Nathan cried, losing his temper somewhat because of the air of authority which this fellow assumed. "'Rebels and sedition-breeders' are names which have too much meaning in these days for you to let them fall so trippingly from your tongue! Have a care, you Tory sneak, lest even while acting the part of guard over your betters, you come to grief! I'm not minded to take many threats from a coward and a spy."

"In this case, however, you will take whatsoever I choose to give, Nathan Shelby, for it needs only that I raise my voice to bring here those who would shoot you down did you so much as lift your hand against me."

"And it is such knowledge which makes you so wondrous brave," Evan said with a laugh of scorn which did more to rouse the young spy's anger than words could have done.

He struggled for an instant to speak; but stammered and hesitated as the blood rushed into his face until, losing the last semblance of patience, he motioned for them to move back toward the window from which they had just come.

"If this is what you mean, we are willing to take our stations here without your running the risk of bursting because of your own sense of importance," Nathan said as he moved back a few paces, Evan following the example. "Have a care, however, that you do not attempt to give such orders as we shall be indisposed to obey, lest it seem as if your authority amounted to nothing."

By this time Ephraim so far regained the mastery over himself as to be able to speak, and he cried in a fury:

"We'll soon see whether you dare disobey, and to that end I will keep you busy for an hour or more, until you have learned that I am really the master. Now then, you rebels, remember that the king's troops are near at hand to shoot you down at the first sign of insubordination, and take good heed to move exactly as I command."

Ephraim straightened his body with a consequential air, and stood for an instant as if reflecting upon how he had best prove his authority, while the two prisoners gazed at him in astonishment that he should thus dare trust himself unarmed alone with them.

"Stand straight and look me in the face!" he commanded. "If the day's march was not enough to break your spirits, we will see what a little exercise will do for you now. Keep step, and travel around this room until I give you permission to stop."

"Do you think we are to be bullied by such as you?" Nathan asked in great astonishment.

"If you think it is wise, refuse to do as I say, and before five minutes have gone by you will learn the result of disobedience."

Neither Evan nor Nathan moved, but stood looking inquiringly into each other's eyes with an expression on their faces which would have warned the Tory of mischief had he been less deeply occupied with his own fancied importance.

"Fall into line and march, or it will be the worse for you!" he cried, advancing threateningly with upraised hand until he was within striking distance of the prisoners, and for an instant it appeared as if he intended to inflict punishment then and there.

Whatever idea may have been in his mind cannot be said, yet it hardly seems possible he would have attempted personal violence while alone with those whom he had wronged, even though the soldiers were so near at hand.

It is certain, however, the boys fully believed he would carry out the implied threat, and without thinking of the possible consequences, or stopping to realize what might be the result if this spy was roughly handled, as if with one accord they leaped upon him, Nathan taking the precaution of clapping his hand over the bully's mouth at the first onset in such manner that it was impossible for him to speak or make an outcry.

Even a stronger lad than Ephraim Sowers would have gone down before this sudden attack as quickly as did he, and in a twinkling the prisoners held him upon the floor in such fashion that only one arm remained free.

Evan sat upon his feet, while Nathan, in addition to covering his mouth, held his right arm firmly.

With his left hand Ephraim struck out to the best of his ability, but without accomplishing anything whatsoever, and he was permitted to thus thrash around, doing no harm to any save himself, until he had been thoroughly wearied by the struggle.

"I reckon we have got time enough to teach you quite a lesson," Nathan whispered with but slight show of anger. "You are supposed to be guarding us prisoners, and the redcoats will give little heed to you for some hours to come. While we are alone you shall get a taste of what you would deal out to others."

As a matter of course Ephraim made no reply, because it was impossible so to do; but his captors could read in his eyes the threats his tongue was powerless to utter.

"I know what you would say, my fine Tory spy. You have in your mind the thought that we must in time let you up, and then it shall be your turn, for the soldiers will be called in to perform what you fail in doing. How well would that plan work if we did our duty, and killed you here and now? It is what should be done to a lad who, having received nothing but favors in this section of the colony, betrays to their death a hundred or more of his neighbors."

Anger had rapidly died out of Ephraim's eyes as Nathan spoke, for by the tone of the latter, one would have said that he was in deadly earnest, and really questioned whether or no it was not his duty to take this worthless life.

"It would not be a hard matter to let his life-blood out," Evan added, intent only on doing his share toward frightening the spy, "and perhaps it will be best even though he had not betrayed Colonel Clarke and his men, for we can have a very fair idea of what he will be, once power is his."

"Find something with which to tie his feet and hands, and then we will contrive a gag so that it is not necessary to sit over him in this fashion."

Evan obeyed the command by tearing from the lad's hunting-shirt two or three strips of material sufficiently stout to resist all his struggles, and in a comparatively short space of time the Tory was bound hand and foot, with one sleeve of his own garment stuffed inside his mouth as a gag.

He was powerless now either to move or speak, and only when the work was accomplished did the boys fully realize that they had, perhaps, injured themselves by thus temporarily turning the tables.

"It would have been better had we let him go his own gait," Evan said in a whisper as he drew Nathan toward the window where the helpless Tory could not overhear his words. "Of course we cannot hope to keep him here longer than morning, and it is hardly likely the redcoats will suffer him to be absent so many hours without making certain he is safe. Once the troopers come we shall suffer for this bit of pleasantry."

"They are not like to put in an appearance for several hours yet, more especially if the villain gave out that he would stand guard until weary of the sport."

"Yet the end must finally come."

Nathan started as if a sudden thought had flashed upon him, and turned quickly toward the window as he seized one of the heavy bars.

"Have you any idea that it might be possible to pull that down?" Evan asked wonderingly.

"Hark you, lad," and now Nathan appeared like one laboring under great excitement. "Why might we not escape? The Britishers will have no care for us while it is believed that sneak is acting as sentinel, and if one of these bars could be removed, we might count on at least an hour's start."

"But there is no hope of our being able to remove the barrier."

"Who shall say until it has been tried?"

"I am certain that with our bare hands we might tug and strain until morning without so much as loosening one of the fastenings."

It was as if this suggestion excited Nathan to a yet more brilliant flight of fancy in the line of escape, for suddenly he darted toward the door where he stood a moment in the attitude of a listener, and then retracing his steps, whispered to Evan:

"It is almost certain the Britishers are on the floor below. This Tory has the key of the door in his pocket——"

"Surely you are not thinking of attempting to make your way down past all those who have taken possession of the house?"

"By no means; yet what will prevent our venturing into some of the chambers nearby, where perchance we shall find what will serve as a lever to remove these bars."

Evan seized his comrade's hands ecstatically. There was every reason to believe such a venture might be made, and without waiting to discuss it he began searching Ephraim's pockets for the key.

This was soon found. A bulky iron instrument fashioned by hand, and mostlike brought from the mother country, it could not well be concealed.

Cautiously, lest the slightest grating of the iron should give the alarm, the boys shot the bolt back; the door was opened, and they were at last free of the upper portion of the house.

It was not safe to loiter in their work, however, for at any moment some one might come from below to ascertain what Ephraim was doing, and the boys moved as swiftly as they did noiselessly until, when hardly more than a minute had elapsed, they had in their possession such tools as it seemed positive would enable them to effect the purpose.

An old musket barrel, and a strip of oak which went to make up a quilting-frame, were the articles which the lads brought into the room, carefully barring the door behind them and replacing the key in Ephraim's pocket.

These implements would serve to pry off the bars of the window, but whether it might be done silently or not was a matter that could only be determined by experiment.

The helpless spy was watching their every movement, and by bending over him now and then the lads could see, even in the gloom, an expression of anger in his eyes.

He must have realized now that the chances in favor of their escape were brought about wholly through his desire to gloat over those whom he believed were in his power.

It can readily be believed, however, that the two lads did not spend much time upon the spy. Had there been a possibility of taking him with them, they would have run many risks in order to accomplish such a purpose; but since that was out of the question, and he powerless for harm during a certain time at least, they could not afford to waste precious moments upon him.

"I will use this bar as a lever, and do you stand by with the musket-barrel to hold such advantage as may be gained," Nathan said. "It is reasonable to suppose there will be some creaking as the nails are forced out; but that we cannot prevent."

"Work as cautiously as may be possible, for we have ample time."

The lower bar was within three inches of the window-ledge, and upon this Nathan determined to direct his efforts, since it would probably be the most easily removed.

The stout quilting-frame was inserted beneath it edgewise, which brought one end some distance into the room, the window-ledge serving as a fulcrum.

Evan stood near at hand, ready with the musket-barrel in case a shorter lever could be used to better advantage, and, after listening for an instant to make certain that none of the enemy were nearabout on the outside, the boys began that work which it was hoped would open the door to freedom.

Slowly and steadily the bar was raised upward as the hand-fashioned nails bent under the strain, and then came a creaking as the iron was drawn through the wood; not loud, but sounding in the ears of the anxious lads to be of such volume that it seemed positive an alarm would be given.

Both ceased their efforts, and stood near the window listening.

No unusual sounds betokened that the redcoats had heard the warning noise.

All was still save for the sounds of revelry in the apartment below, and the hum of the soldiers' voices nearabout the stables on the other side of the dwelling.

"Try it again," Evan whispered with feverish eagerness. "We have raised it half an inch already, and as much more of a strain will leave it in such shape that it can be readily pushed aside."

Nathan did as his comrade suggested, and save for a slight creaking now and then, the work was carried on in almost perfect silence until the bar hung only by the points of the nails.

It remained simply to force it outward with their hands, at the same time preventing it from falling to the ground.

With this removed, the aperture would be sufficiently large to admit of their crawling through, and the time had come, thanks to the spy who would have taken their lives had his power been sufficient, that they might follow on the trail of Sarah Dillard to Greene's Spring, if her mad ride had not led her to death elsewhere.

"There is no reason why we should waste any time here," Evan said hurriedly, nervous now that the moment for action had arrived. "The redcoats may come at any moment to see how their spy is faring, and it would be a grievous disappointment to find ourselves checked at the instant when it seems as if we were freed."

"I have got just one word to say to that Tory villain, and then I am ready," Nathan replied. "Do you push off the bar, taking good care that it does not drop from your hands, while I warn him of what will surely be his fate if he continues on the road he has chosen."

Evan acted upon this suggestion as Nathan kneeled by the side of Ephraim and whispered:

"You can have the satisfaction of knowing that we would yet be fast prisoners but for your having come to bully us. Until the moment you threatened to strike I had no idea escape would be possible; but the opportunity has arrived, and we shall take advantage of it. Now hark you, Master Sowers, and remember all I say, for there be more than Evan and I who will carry out this threat. Continue your spying upon the Americans, serve the Britisherslonger, and you shall be marked for what may be worse than death. When the life of such as you is necessary in the cause of freedom no one would hesitate to take it, coward and sneak though you be. Turn about from your ways this moment, or expect that the hand of every Mountain Man and every American soldier will be against you."

Ephraim twisted about as if it would have pleased him right well could he have spoken at that moment, but the gag choked his words, and he perforce remained silent however much he would have liked to use his voice.

Then all was ready for the flight.

The bar had been removed, and Evan stood beside the window impatient to be off, fearing each instant lest one of the enemy should ascend the stairs.

"Go you ahead," Nathan whispered, "and if when you reach the ground the redcoats appear, do your best to make good your escape, thinking not of me."

"I will never desert a comrade."

"You must in this case, if it so be opportunity for flight presents itself. It is not your life nor mine, Evan, which is of moment now. We must remember only those who are in such great peril, for I have many doubts as to whether Sarah Dillard can force that colt over the mountain road. Hesitate no longer; but set out, and from this instant cease to think of anything save that you are to arrive at Colonel Clarke's encampment without loss of time."

Thus urged, Evan delayed no longer than was necessary, but a certain number of seconds were spent in the effort to force his body through the narrow aperture, because of the awkward position which the circumstances demanded.

With Nathan's help he pushed his feet through first, and when half his body was outside, allowed himself to slip down at the expense of severe scratching from the bar, which yet remained in position above, until he hung by his hands on the window-ledge.

"The distance is not great," Nathan whispered encouragingly, "and you should be able to drop without making much noise. Do not speak once you are on the ground; but get behind the smaller stable as soon as may be, and if in five minutes I do not join you, push on toward Greene's Spring alone."

"You will not delay?"

"Not so much as a minute. Now drop."

A slight jar, such as might have been made by a child leaping from a height of ten feet, was all that came back to the anxious listener at the window to tell of his comrade's movements, and then he in turn set about following the example.

Now it was that Ephraim made strenuous efforts to free himself.

He writhed to and fro on the floor as if bending all his energies to break the bonds which confined his limbs, and so fearful was Nathan lest the Tory spy should succeed in his purpose, that he turned back to make certain the boy was yet helpless.

"I am almost tempted to pay off the score 'twixt you and I before leaving; but it would be cowardly to strike one who is helpless, I suppose," the lad said half to himself, and then turned resolutely, as if finding it difficult to resist the temptation, setting off on the road to freedom.

It was not as easy to force himself out between the ledge and the bar as in the case of Evan, because of his being considerably larger, and the clothing was literally torn from his back before he was finally in a position where nothing more was required than to drop to the ground.

It appeared to him as if he made double as much noise as had his comrade, and before daring to creep across the stable-yard to the rendezvous agreed upon, he remained several seconds on the alert for the slightest sound betokening the movements of the Britishers.

No unusual noise came upon his ear, and saying to himself that it was hardly possible he and Evan had succeeded in making their escape with so little difficulty, he pushed cautiously forward until, when he was within the gloom of the building, his comrade seized him by the hands.

This was no time for conversation, nor was it the place in which to loiter. Advantage must be taken of every second from this instant until they had carried the warning to Colonel Clarke's men, or learned that Sarah Dillard had succeeded in her ride, and Nathan pressed Evan's hand in token that they should push forward without delay.

The direct trail was well defined, and the boys struck into it an hundred yards or more from the stable, when Nathan whispered triumphantly:

"Now that we have succeeded in making our escape, Evan, it is only a question of endurance, and we must not think of self until after having met Sarah Dillard, or had speech with Colonel Clarke."

CHAPTER V.

SARAH DILLARD.

Nathan and Evan had good cause for self-congratulations.

The escape had been accomplished almost as if the enemy themselves contributed to its success, and so long as the two remained within earshot of the plantation, nothing was heard to betoken that their flight had been discovered.

Thanks to the fact that Ephraim Sowers had taken it upon himself to wreak a little private revenge simply because the lads had discovered his true nature, the Britishers would rest content, believing their prisoners were secure under his guard, and it might be several hours before any member of Major Ferguson's party had sufficient curiosity to inquire regarding the young Tory's absence.

Unless, perchance, he was to act as guide for the party who would march to Greene's Spring, neither Englishman nor Tory would have use for the spy before daylight, and it was quite within the range of possibility that he might remain gagged and bound upon the floor of the improvised prison until the troop was ready to resume the march next morning.

Once they were clear of the dwelling Nathan and Evan wasted little thought on Ephraim.

When the time should come that they might make known his true character among those who had befriended the lad, then would they remember him to some purpose; but while they were pressing forward through the thicket at full speed, now catching a glimpse of the footprints of Sarah Dillard's horse, and again being convinced that he had left the trail, it was as if Ephraim had no existence.

Many times before the first three miles of distance had been traversed did they speculate as to the probable time when Major Ferguson would send forward those men who were to butcher or capture the little band of Americans at the Spring; but without arriving at any definite conclusion.

From the Dillard plantation to the encampment concerning which Ephraim had given information, was no less than twenty miles, and in case the horsemen should be selected to do the bloody work, about three hours would be required for the journey.

If the foot-soldiers were chosen for the task, then six hours would be none too long; but neither of the boys believed the infantry would take part in the proposed maneuver, otherwise the men would most likely have set out before dark.

"We can hold certain that the horsemen will make the attack, and I am guessing they will not start before eleven o'clock to-night. They may then fall upon our men between two and three in the morning, when it is said sleep weighs heaviest upon the eyelids, and if neither Sarah Dillard nor we succeed in getting through to give the alarm, there is little doubt but that all under Colonel Clarke's command will fall victims."

"We must get through," Evan cried with energy, and Nathan added:

"We shall do it, lad; never you fear, for there is like to be nothing that can stop us, unless by some unfortunate chance the troopers begin their journey before we have reckoned on."

Then once more the boys trudged on in silence until, perhaps ten minutes later, they were brought to a sudden standstill by sounds in the distance which seemed to proclaim the movement of some heavy body through the underbrush.

Unarmed as they were, flight was their only defence, and the two bent forward in the attitude of listeners, keenly on the alert for the first indication as to the character of this noisy traveler.

At one moment Nathan would announce positively that the disturbance was caused by some animal, and again he felt equally certain he could hear in the distance the sound of human voices.

"There is only one thing of which I am fully convinced," he said after being thus forced to change his opinion several times. "Whoever may be out there yonder is a stranger in this section of the colony, otherwise he would be more careful in proclaiming his whereabouts in such fashion."

"In that case we may safely venture to creep up nearer," Evan suggested. "So far as I can make out, that disturber of the peace neither lessens nor increases his distance, and we might wait here until the troopers come up without being any the wiser."

To this Nathan agreed, and the two advanced cautiously pace by pace until suddenly, and at the same instant, a low exclamation of surprise burst from the lips of both.

They had recognized Sarah Dillard's voice, and knew without waiting for further proof that her mad ride had come to a sudden and untimely end.

Now the two pressed forward at a run, slackening not the pace until they were where such a view could be had of the struggling animal and the courageous woman as was possible in the gloom.

"Who is it?" she called, hearing the advance of the boys, and there was a ring of alarm in her tone which told that she feared the redcoats might have pushed forward to make the attack.

"It is Nathan Shelby and Evan McDowells," the former cried, and gained some idea of the good woman's surprise when she failed for a moment to speak.

"Step out here where I may see you; but take care not to further alarm the colt," she said, distrusting the announcement even though she recognized the voice.

The boys obeyed, and when Mrs. Dillard had the proof of her own eyes as to their identity, she demanded to be told how they had succeeded in escaping.

"The Britishers must have left the plantation, otherwise how could you be here?"

"If Major Ferguson's troop had gone we should have been forced to accompany them, else Ephraim Sowers has less influence than he believes."

Then, without waiting for further questioning, and in as few words as possible, Nathan explained all, so far as he knew, that had taken place at the plantation immediately after the departure of Mrs. Dillard, asking as he concluded the story:

"Was it not possible for you to keep the colt on the trail?"

"He threw me when he got nearabout this point; but I contrived to retain hold of the bridle, and have kept him with me, although thus far it has availed me little, since I am unable to remount."

"Suppose you let either Evan or I ride him? There will be less likelihood of his throwing one of us."

"I question if you could come so near doing it as I can, for he is acquainted with me, and would not allow either of you to approach him."

"I can ride any horse that another can bridle," Nathan replied confidently, as he went toward the colt, who during this brief conversation had been standing comparatively quiet.

It was much as if he had heard the rash assertion, and was determined to prove it false, for the boy had no sooner begun to advance than he reared and plunged in such a frantic manner that Mrs. Dillard well-nigh lost her hold of the bridle.

"It is useless for you to attempt it," she said as soon as the animal had quieted down somewhat. "He has been accustomed to no one but me, and because I had been able to lead him by the halter, did I venture to put on the bridle."

"There seems little chance you will be able to mount," Evan said after a brief pause, "and every moment increases the danger to those at Greene's Spring. No one can say how soon the Britishers may set out, and there are not less than eighteen miles to be traversed."

"I know it," Mrs. Dillard cried like one nearly frantic with apprehension. "I know it, and yet what may be done? It is certain neither of you boys can come as near managing the horse as I, and yet, I am unable to remount."

"Would you venture to lead him back?"

"To what end?"

"Evan and I might push forward on foot, trusting to getting through in time."

"And there is little chance you could succeed, lads. Eighteen miles over this rough road would require certainly no less than six hours, and before that time has passed the redcoats must have overtaken you."

Then Mrs. Dillard turned her attention to soothing the colt, and during five minutes or more the boys waited with ill-concealed impatience as he alternately advanced to receive her caresses, and then reared and plunged when she attempted to throw her arm over his neck.

"It is better we push ahead, trusting to the poor chance of arriving in time, than to stand here idle," Nathan said at length. "I do not believe you could force him to keep the trail even though you succeed in remounting."

"It must be done," Mrs. Dillard cried sharply. "There is no other means by which we may be certain of warning those who are in danger, and the colt shall be made to perform his part."

"How can we help you?"

The anxious woman looked about her an instant as if trying to decide how the task might be accomplished, and then she said in the tone of one who ventures upon an experiment:

"Suppose you two come up gently toward him, one on each side, with the idea of seizing him by the bridle. If that could be done, and you were able to hold him a few seconds, I promise to get upon his back."

"And perhaps only to have your brains dashed out the next instant."

"There is no reason why we should speculate as to the result. I must mount him, boys, and he must be made to go forward. It is our only hope, and when so many lives hang in the balance it surely seems as if the good Lord would permit that I should do what at this moment appears to be impossible."

Neither Evan nor Nathan believed they could on foot traverse the distance which lay between them and Greene's Spring before the Britishers should arrive, and yet at the same time they had little hope the restive animal would be brought into submission; but at the moment it seemed to be the only alternative, and without delay they set about acting upon Mrs. Dillard's suggestion.

Making a short detour through the bushes, they came up on his flank, on either side, while the animal reared and plunged until it seemed certain he would shake off the woman's hold upon the bridle. Then with a sudden dash both boys gained his head at the same instant, and this much of the work was accomplished.

Now the animal redoubled his efforts to escape, frightened by the touch of strangers; but the boys held bravely on, at times raised high from the ground, until it became a question as to whether the bridle would stand the strain which was put upon it.

"Don't let go," Nathan cried as the colt made a more furious leap, forcing Evan to jump quickly aside lest he be struck by the animal's hoofs. "Don't let go, and we may possibly so far tire him out that Mrs. Dillard can mount."

"She could not ride this beast even though he was saddled," Evan muttered, now losing all hope that the message might be delivered in time.

During such while as the boys had been struggling with the colt, Mrs. Dillard stood dangerously near his flanks, watching for an opportunity, and Evan had no more than uttered his gloomy prediction when, clutching the animal's mane with her left hand, she vaulted on to his back, seizing the bridle as she leaped.

"Now if you can head him up the trail, you may let go," she said hurriedly; but Nathan was not minded Captain Dillard's wife should ride to what seemed almost certain death without another protest from him.

"The colt is maddened by his struggles with us, and in far more dangerous a condition than when you first mounted. It is madness to think of attempting to make your way through the thicket in the darkness. I implore you to give over the attempt, and let us press on as best we may afoot."

"Now you are asking that I leave these brave men, and among them my husband, to be surprised by an enemy that knows no mercy, for it is positive you could not get through in time. Turn the colt, if it so be you can, and once he is headed in the right direction, jump aside."

"Shall we do it?" Evan asked, for even now it was in his mind to disobey the brave woman's commands.

 "Ay, I see no other course," Nathan replied, and then he devoted all his energies toward carrying out her instructions.

Not less than five minutes were spent in the battle between the boys and the animal, and then the former were the conquerers so far as having turned him around was concerned.

"Now stand ready to let him go, and leap back out of the way," Mrs. Dillard cried. "Then do you press on at your best speed in case I am thrown again, and forced to give over this method of traveling."

"Are you ready?" Evan cried.

"Ay, when you say the word."

"Let go!"

As the boys leaped back the colt darted forward at full speed, wildly lashing out with his hind feet, and in a twinkling the animal and his rider were lost to view in the gloom.

"She will have earned Captain Dillard's life, whether it be saved or not; but it will be at the expense of her own, for there is not a man in the Carolinas who can keep that beast on this mountain trail."

"It would have been better if we had not met her," Evan said gloomily, "for then she would have been forced to go back, instead of riding to her death as she is now doing."

To this Nathan made no reply, and while one might have counted twenty the two lads stood on the trail in the darkness as if there was nothing more for them to do this night.

It was Evan who first aroused himself to a full realization of the situation, and he said, much like one who awakes from a troubled dream:

"It is not for us to waste precious time here, Nathan. Believing that Sarah Dillard cannot gain Greene's Spring, we must press forward at the best of our ability, for there is a slight hope we may arrive in time to give the alarm, although it hardly seems possible at this moment."

"You are right, Evan, and from this instant there shall be no halting," Nathan cried, as he set out with a regular, swinging gait, which promised to carry him at a speed of not less than three miles an hour.

Now, being fully convinced that the safety of Colonel Clarke's men depended entirely upon themselves, they hastened onward without thought of fatigue, making no halt save now and then when they stopped to refresh themselves with water from a mountain stream.

The gloom was now so dark that it was impossible to distinguish any imprints on the trail, and, consequently, the lads could form no idea as to whether Sarah Dillard was yet keeping in the direct course, or if the colt swerved from one side to the other, carrying her amid the underbrush, where she must inevitably be killed. Until they believed midnight was come Nathan and Evan had pressed steadily forward, and then came that sound which told them all their efforts were vain.

From the rear could be heard faintly the sound of horses' hoofs, and involuntarily the two halted.

"The Britishers are coming!" Evan whispered, and Nathan's voice was tremulous as he replied:

"They started even sooner than I feared, and all our efforts are vain so far, for it is not less than six miles from here to Greene's Spring."

"And our friends will be butchered!"

"There is hardly one chance in a hundred but that the surprise will be complete, in which case we know what must be the result."

They had ceased to believe in even the possibility that Sarah Dillard might have accomplished the journey in safety, and accepted it as a fact that the plans of the enemy, laid on information brought by Ephraim Sowers, would be carried through successfully.

Nearer and nearer came the horsemen until the two lads could hear the hum of conversation among the men before they realized the necessity of concealing themselves.

No good could be accomplished, so far as those at Greene's Spring were concerned, by their capture, and it was reasonable to suppose much harm might come to themselves after they were carried back to where Ephraim Sowers might wreak his vengeance upon them.

Until this evening the young Tory had had no cause for enmity save on account of their having discovered his true character; but now, after remaining gagged and bound a certain number of hours, he must be panting for revenge, and it might be that Major Ferguson would not check him.

So long had they thus remained as if dazed that there was hardly time to conceal themselves in the underbrush a few feet distant from the trail before the foremost of the horsemen came into view.

The enemy were riding in couples, and from his hiding-place Evan counted ninety pairs of riders before the whole of the troop had passed.

Then it seemed as if fortune was determined to play her most scurvy trick upon these two lads, whose one desire was to save the lives of their friends.

Evan, who had crouched on one knee when he first sank behind the bushes, endeavored to change his position in order to relieve the strain upon his limb, and by so doing slipped on a rotten branch, which broke beneath his weight with a report seemingly as loud as that of a pistol-shot.

Instantly the troopers halted immediately opposite, and before the boys could have taken refuge in flight, two having dismounted, plunged into the underbrush.

All this had been done so quickly that the fugitives literally had no time to flee, and hardly more than thirty seconds elapsed from the breaking of the twig until each lad was held roughly and firmly in the clutch of a soldier.

"What's wrong in there?" an officer from the trail shouted, and one of the captors replied as he dragged his prey out into the open:

"We have found a couple of young rebels, and they look much like the two we left behind us at the plantation."

Word was passed ahead for the entire troop to halt, and an officer whom the boys afterward recognized as a Tory by the name of Dunlap, who held the king's commission as colonel, came riding back.

"Who are you?" he asked as the troopers forced their prisoners in front of them on the trail where they might most readily be seen.

"Nathan Shelby and Evan McDowells."

"How is it you are here? Are you not the same who were taken prisoners this evening and confined in the Dillard house?"

"We are," Nathan replied without hesitation.

"How did you escape?"

"Ephraim Sowers was sent, or came of his own will, to make us march around the room by way of punishment."

"No such orders as that could have been given by Major Ferguson."

"I know not how that may be; but Ephraim acted the part of jailer, and commanded us to do his bidding, which was none other than that we march around the room even though we had been afoot all day."

"That doesn't explain how you escaped?"

"Ephraim was unarmed, but threatened to strike us when we refused. The result was the same as if almost any one else had been in our position. We made Ephraim a prisoner, and then, by forcing off one of the wooden bars, slipped out of the window."

"Then the boy is yet there?" the colonel said, as if in surprise that such should be the case.

"Ay, if he has not been released. We left him safely enough."

Nathan believed that he and Evan would be roughly treated so soon as that which they had done was made known; but the troopers appeared to think it a laughing matter, and even the colonel who was in charge of the detachment did not look upon it with any great degree of severity, for he said after a brief pause:

"Ephraim must remain where he is until our return, and perhaps after this night he will be more careful when he puts himself into the power of his enemies. You who have taken the prisoners shall guard them until we have finished our work, and then it is likely we will have more to keep them company. Mount, and see to it that the rebels do not make their escape again."

The troopers obeyed, pulling the two lads after them into the saddle, with many a threat as to what would be the result if there was any resistance, until Nathan said, but without show of temper or impatience:

"We are willing to ride, and shall not be so foolish as to resist when the odds are so strongly against us."

"We are not in the humor to put up with any more rebel tricks this night, and at the first show of an attempt to escape I shall use my knife in a way that won't be pleasant," the trooper replied as he put spurs to his horse, and the detachment rode three or four miles further before slackening pace.

Then they were come in the vicinity of Greene's Spring, and the boys who had already braved so much in the hope of being able to warn their friends in danger, believed that the time was very near at hand when they must perforce see Colonel Clarke's men ruthlessly cut down or captured.

CHAPTER VI.

GREENE'S SPRING.

Many wild plans came into Nathan's mind during the short time the main body of the detachment were halted while skirmishers went ahead to ascertain if Ephraim had correctly described the situation of affairs.

It seemed to him at this moment as if he must do something toward warning the friends of freedom of the danger which menaced, and was ready to act, whatever might be the cost to him.

Once he said to himself that he would wait until they were come nigh to the encampment, and then he and Evan should cry aloud at the full strength of their lungs, even though the Britishers killed them an instant later—their lives would count for but little if these others who were so necessary to the colonists might be saved.

A moment's reflection served to convince him that such a plan was impracticable, and in casting it aside he came to believe that possibly he and Evan might succeed in getting hold of one of the troopers' muskets sufficiently long to discharge it.

Anything which would make noise enough to arouse the sleeping men might answer his purpose, and yet he racked his brain in vain to hit upon that which should give promise of being successful.

Neither he nor Evan had an opportunity for private conversation. The two troopers held the lads six or eight feet from each other, as if suspecting they might plot mischief if allowed freedom of speech, and therefore it was they had no opportunity of comparing plans which had for their end only the welfare of Colonel Clarke's forces.

At the expiration of ten minutes word was passed along the line for the men to advance slowly, and every precaution was taken as the command was obeyed, to prevent even so much as the rattle of their accoutrements, lest by such means the Americans be apprised of the horrible fate in store for them.

Soon the detachment was come within a quarter of a mile, as nearly as Evan and Nathan could judge, of the spot Colonel Clarke had selected for the encampment, and now no man spoke above a whisper.

"This is serious business on which we are bent this night," the trooper who held Nathan captive whispered threateningly, and standing so near Evan that he also might overhear the words, "and the lives of two boys like you would not be allowed to come betwixt us and our purpose. Therefore take heed, lads, that our orders are to kill you in cold blood rather than allow any alarm to be given. Now if it so chanced that you struck your foot against my musket, or shouted, or did anything to break the silence, I should consider it my duty to obey the commands, and as soon as might be one or both of you would be past all danger. Take an old soldier's advice, and make the best of a bad matter. It is no longer possible you can warn your friends, and the most you could accomplish would be your own death."

There was little need for the trooper to make this plain statement of the situation, for both the boys understood full well how summarily they would be dealt with in case they failed to obey any orders given by the men.

Now whispered commands came down the line for the soldiers to dismount, and for every fifth trooper to remain in the rear to care for the horses.

When this command had been obeyed, and the animals tied with their heads together in groups of five, it was found that the man who held Evan prisoner was thus detailed to care for the animals, while his comrade belonged to the force which would advance.

Therefore it was that Nathan's captor turned him over to the other trooper, saying as he did so:

"If you have any doubts as to being able to keep these young rebels in proper subjection, I will truss them up before leaving; but it seems to me one Englishman can care for five horses and two boys, without any very great amount of difficulty."

"I am not afraid but that it can be done after some sort of fashion, yet I had rather not kill a lad even though he be a rebel, so if it is all the same to you, pass a couple of those saddle-straps over their arms, and I'll be more certain of keeping them here without using a bullet."

The trooper did as he was requested, and the boys were fettered in such a manner as precluded all possibility of escape.

With both arms stretched to their sides flight was out of the question, and the hearts of the lads were heavy in their breasts, for they must remain in the rear while the redcoats went on to do the slaughtering.

"I could kill Ephraim Sowers and never believe I had committed a murder," Nathan whispered when the two, placed back to back, were fastened to a convenient tree. "All the blood spilled this night will be upon his head, and that brave men should meet their death through such as him makes it all the more pitiful."

"There is a chance Sarah Dillard succeeded in getting through to the Spring," Evan whispered in a tremulous tone.

"I cannot believe it. The captain himself would never have made such a doubtful venture, and surely a woman could not succeed where he must have failed."

Now those of the troopers who had not been detailed to the care of the horses, were ordered forward, and soon only the animals, with perhaps twenty men to guard them, remained in this portion of the thicket.

Not a sound betrayed the movements of the redcoats as they advanced to do what seemed little less than murder.

Even the boys, knowing how many were making their way through the underbrush, listened in vain for the slightest noise which should tell of the progress. A band of Indians could hardly have moved more stealthily, and unless the members of the little encampment were already on the alert, the doom of all was sealed.

The suspense of the boys became so great as the moments passed that they could not carry on a conversation. Speculations were vain when in a few seconds the dreadful reality would be upon them, and their hearts beat so violently that it was as if the blood must burst from their veins.

The seconds passed like moments, and yet all too swiftly as the lads realized what time must bring to their friends.

It seemed to Nathan as if they had remained there silent and motionless fully an hour listening for the first sound of the conflict, or the massacre, whichever it might be, and yet all was as silent as when the troopers left.

He began to fancy that both Sarah Dillard and Ephraim Sowers had been mistaken in believing Colonel Clarke's men were encamped at the Spring, and when this thought had grown in his mind until it was almost a well-defined hope, the first musket-shot rang out.

"The murderers have begun," he said to his comrade in a voice so choked by emotion that the words sounded strange and indistinct.

Then came a volley—a second and a third, and the troopers who held the horses started in astonishment, perhaps fear, for this was not the absolute surprise on which they had counted.

Now the rattle of musketry increased until there could be no question but that it was a conflict, and not a massacre, which was taking place.

By some means the patriots had been warned in due season, and were ready to meet the foe, as they ever had been.

"It is Sarah Dillard's ride that has saved them!" Evan exclaimed as if questioning the truth of his own statement, and straightway Nathan fell to weeping, so great was the relief which came upon him as he realized that the friends of freedom had been prepared for the foe.

The troopers nearabout the boys were so excited and astonished, because what they had counted on as being a complete surprise proved to have been a failure, that no one heard Evan's remark, and the prisoners could have shouted for very joy when the men began speculating one with the other as to how word might have been sent to the patriots.

"It is certain they were ready to receive us," one man said as if in anger because the plan was miscarrying. "That firing is being done by men who were ready for battle as were ours. There has been a traitor in the camp."

"How might that be?" another asked fiercely. "At the last halting-place we were twenty miles from the rebel encampment, and certain it is no one could have ridden ahead of us."

"These two boy did succeed in escaping, despite the fact that Major Ferguson believed them to be safe in the chamber of the dwelling."

"Ay; but what does that prove? We overtook them on the way, and surely you cannot claim that they might have walked twenty miles from the time of escaping until they were recaptured?"

The rattle of musketry increased, and to the eager ears of the boys it seemed as if the noise of the conflict was approaching, which would indicate that the Britishers were being driven back.

"Does it appear to you as if we heard those sounds more clearly?" Nathan asked, hoping he had not been mistaken, and yet feeling almost certain the patriots could do but little more than hold their own.

"I am positive of it!" Evan cried with a ring of joy and triumph in his tone. "Now and then I can hear voices even amid the tumult, and that was impossible five minutes ago."

One of the troopers, overhearing this remark, said to his comrade gloomily:

"The rebels are getting the best of us, who counted on taking them completely by surprise."

"There is no doubt of that," the other soldier replied, and straightway the men began making the horses ready for departure, as if they expected their comrades would come back in full flight, and need the means of continuing it.

When five minutes more had passed there was no longer any question as to the result of the combat.

By this time the British were so near where the horses had been left that now and then stray bullets whistled among the branches above the heads of the prisoners, and the two lads began debating how it might be possible for them to escape when the troop should be in full flight.

However kind Fortune had been to the Americans on this night, she was not so indulgent as to give the lads their liberty.

As could be told from the rattle of musketry, the British made a stand after fifteen minutes' or more of hot fighting, and the Americans, having accomplished as much, and, perhaps, even more than they had expected, were willing the invaders should draw off if such was their disposition.

In less than half an hour from the time they set out to massacre the supposedly sleeping encampment, the redcoats had returned, and, standing by their horses, awaiting the command to mount. Now it was that even in the gloom the boys could see how many of the animals were without riders.

There had been no empty saddles when the troop rode up, and now on looking around there was hardly a squad of horses where more than two out of five had a man standing by his side.

"The slaughter was not wholly among our friends," Evan whispered to Nathan, and the latter, bent only on trying to escape, said hurriedly:

"Think of nothing but yourself just now. There must be a chance for us to give them the slip amid all this confusion."

He had no more than spoken before one of the officers came up and asked of those standing near by:

"Who had charge of these lads?"

The two troopers who had made the capture replied to the question, and then came the order:

"See to it that you hold them fast. There is no reason why your own beasts should carry double while there are so many spare horses; but lash them firmly to the saddles, for Major Ferguson must have speech with them by daylight."

"We are to suffer because the Britishers have been repulsed," Evan whispered, and Nathan replied manfully:

"Much can be endured, knowing as we do all that has taken place this night. While I am not hankering to come into the power of Ephraim Sowers again, as most like we shall, it will be less painful now this bloody plan has gone awry."

Considerable time was spent before the remnants of the detachment began the return march.

There were many wounded to be cared for, and a number so badly injured that they must remain behind. Some of the dead were to be buried, and the soldiers who had fallen nearest the encampment must have the last office performed for them by those whom they would have massacred.

Finally all was in readiness.

Nathan and Evan, each on a trooper's horse with his feet tied beneath the saddle, were given a place just in advance of their captors and about midway of the troop.

Colonel Dunlap and his officers set out in advance.

The command to "march" was given, and the crestfallen redcoats turned their faces toward Captain Dillard's plantation.

Now it was impossible for the prisoners to speak one with the other; during four hours they endured a most painful journey, bound in such manner that their limbs became cramped, and it was as if all the blood in their bodies had been forced toward their heads.

The lads were hardly conscious during the last hour of that painful march, and when, arriving at the plantation, the ropes were unloosed, they would have fallen to the ground but for the assistance of those who guarded them.

Ephraim Sowers was awaiting the return of those who had gone out because of the information he brought, and he gave vent to a loud cry of vindictive joy when he saw them bringing the two he most desired to see.

He was near at hand when the prisoners reeled helplessly in the saddles, and as they were laid upon the ground the young spy advanced as if to kick them; but was forced back by one of the soldiers, who said sharply:

"None of that, you young renegade. We who wear the king's uniform are not a band of painted savages; but men who fight fairly, never disgrace themselves by striking a helpless or an unarmed man."

"These rebels belong to me. I was in charge of them when they escaped, and shall work my will on them!" Ephraim cried in a rage as he attempted to force himself past the soldier.

"Not while I am standing nearby, unless you have Major Ferguson's written permission, and that I much misdoubt you will get."

It was useless for Ephraim to insist that these lads were his special property, and after learning that some of the men looked with favor upon his intention of torturing them as punishment for their having escaped, he went post haste to the commander.

Some of the redcoats had given the prisoners water, and in a short time they revived sufficiently to be conscious of all that was going on about them.

It was at the moment Ephraim returned that they sat upright, and to their surprise he made no attack upon them, but contented himself by saying threateningly:

"Before this day comes to an end I will have got even with you for last night's work, and you may be certain I shall settle the score with full measure."

"Since you failed in sending death to those at Greene's Spring, we can well afford to listen to your threats," Nathan replied, and then refused to so much as look toward the spy.

From the fact that Ephraim lingered nearby it seemed positive he must have received some promise regarding the custody of the prisoners from Major Ferguson; but yet as the time passed he made no effort to interfere with them, and when the detachment had been at the plantation an hour or more, a messenger came with orders that the two lads be taken into the house, where the commander would have speech with them.

"Now has come the time when we shall see how far that Tory sneak may be allowed to go," Nathan whispered to his comrade. "Do not give him the satisfaction of knowing that we suffer, whatever he may find an opportunity of doing."

"I shall keep my thoughts on Sarah Dillard's ride and its result, and then all pain will be blunted," Evan replied, after which the two followed limpingly (for the blood was not yet circulating properly in their veins) the messenger who had come for them.

Major Ferguson, Colonel Dunlap, Captain Depuyster, and four or five other officers were in the dining-room of Captain Dillard's home when the boys entered, and from the conversation which was being had at that moment Nathan believed they were discussing the question of how Colonel Clarke might have been warned.

This supposition seemed to be correct when the major asked abruptly:

"After you lads escaped from this building, did you meet any one on the road to Greene's Spring?"

For an instant Nathan hesitated to tell that which was a falsehood; but it must be done unless he would betray the woman whose brave ride of the night previous had saved so many lives, and there was only the slightest pause before he replied:

"From the time we got away from Ephraim Sowers until your men recaptured us, we saw no person save those who belonged to the plantation."

"When did you last see the mistress of the house, Mrs. Dillard?"

"We saw her when we were taken upstairs."

"Did you have any further communication with her?"

"She spoke with us while we were in the room—she standing on the outside of the locked door."

"Will you swear that she did not enter the room?"

"Yes; for if she had been able to do that much, I have no doubt she would have aided us to escape."

"Did you have no assistance when you got out of the room which had been converted into a prison?"

"None except from your spy, Ephraim Sowers," Nathan replied, and then he told of the circumstances of the affair, showing that but for the young Tory's vindictiveness the boys would yet have remained in confinement.

"Will you swear that you sent no word to Colonel Clarke's forces?"

"Yes, sir," both the lads replied at the same instant, and with such emphasis that there could be no question but that they were telling the truth.

Then the officer questioned them concerning where they would have gone but for having been overtaken by the troopers; inquired concerning their families, and such other seemingly unimportant matters, to all of which they gave truthful replies.

Perhaps twenty minutes had thus been spent when Major Ferguson turned his head from them as if the interview was at an end, and Nathan, with a mind fully made up to make known the threats in which Ephraim had indulged, asked:

"Is it to be, sir, that the boy who would have ill-treated us when we were supposed to be powerless, will have an opportunity now to take his revenge?"

"Who gave you to understand anything of the kind?"

"He himself, sir. He has already boasted that we shall suffer for what we did to him, although it was no more than one soldier might do to another. He was in our power, and we could have abused him; yet we stayed our hands, save so far as to put him in such condition that an alarm could not be given."

"I ought to have you hanged offhand."

"But we have done nothing, sir, save to escape from one who would have tortured us."

"You are rebels, and that is sufficient reason why you merit death; but there is work I would have you do, and for that reason your lives will be spared. I wish to send a message to all those rebels round about who are now in arms against the king, and if you swear to faithfully repeat my words, you shall go free from this plantation within an hour."

The boys could hardly believe their ears were not deceiving them.

That they should be set free at so small a price, and in face of all the threats Ephraim Sowers had made, was news so joyful as to be incredible, and their astonishment was such that neither made reply until the major asked impatiently:

"Well, well, do you refuse to do even that much in order to earn your liberty?"

"Indeed we do not, sir," Nathan cried eagerly. "We are willing to repeat whatsoever you desire, and to as many as you shall say, no matter how far it may be necessary to travel."

"Are you acquainted with all the rebel leaders hereabouts?"

"With nearly all of them, sir; and I promise that Captain Dillard, Colonel McDowells, or Colonel Campbell—all three gentlemen with whom we have acquaintance—will put us on the way to find those others in this section."

"And you swear faithfully to repeat every word of the message I give you, to each of those rebels who is in command of a dozen or more men?"

"Yes, sir."

"Mind, I am saying that you deserve to be hanged; but at the same time I am in need of messengers, and believe that even though you are among the enemies to the king, I can trust you two."

"We will perform all that we promise, sir."

"And see to it that you do. I am sent into this portion of the Carolinas by General Cornwallis to crush the spirit of rebellion, and here I shall stay until my work be finished. Therefore if you lads attempt to play me false there will come a reckoning, for we shall meet again."

"Even though we be rebels in the sight of the king, we hold to our word, and that both of us have given. We will swear to it in whatsoever manner may be most convincing to you, sir."

"I shall take your word, knowing that the time will speedily come when I can punish you to the fullest extent if you break it. Now say to all the rebels in and about this section of the colonies, even though you are forced to travel many a day, that I have come from General Cornwallis' army unhampered by any orders other than those to crush out the spirit of rebellion, and that if they do not desist from their armed resistance to the king's commands and take protection under my standard, I will march my army over the mountains, hang their leaders, and lay waste their country with fire and sword."

These words he required the boys to repeat for him twice over, and that done, he added:

"Remember what will be the result if you attempt to deceive me. Now go, and see to it that you rest not until the message be delivered to all those in rebellion within a circle of fifty miles. Captain Depuyster, will you take care that they have safe conduct outside our line of sentinels. If the boy Sowers chooses to follow them in the hope of getting his revenge, it will not be in my power to prevent him."

Then with a gesture Nathan and Evan were dismissed, and they walked out of the room as if in a daze, for it did not seem to them possible they had thus been dismissed from captivity.

CHAPTER VII.

AT WATUGA.

Captain Depuyster, who had been charged by Major Ferguson with seeing that the boys were passed through the line of sentinels surrounding the encampment, lingered behind for a moment to speak with the commander, and the newly-released prisoners were still in such a maze of bewilderment at having been given their liberty that they failed to realize there might be necessity for a captain's escort.

They went out of the dwelling, past the sentinels at the door in silence; it was as if neither dared to speak lest the sound of his voice might cause the British commander to reconsider his determination.

Without so much as looking behind them to learn if Captain Depuyster was following, for as a matter of fact they hardly heard the command which Major Ferguson gave relative to their departure, they went straight from the door toward the trail which led to Greene's Spring; but before having advanced twenty paces they were brought to a halt as Ephraim Sowers stepped in front of them.

"Have a care you rebels!" the Tory cried threateningly. "Don't get the idea that you can run away whenever the fancy takes you, for I am not to be caught at a disadvantage every hour in the day, as I was last night."

"If we come in contact with you again there will be more damage done than when we contented ourselves with making you prisoner," Nathan said sharply. "Stand aside, or it will be the worse for you."

Ephraim looked up in surprise that the prisoners should have retained such an independent bearing after their interview with the major, for he counted upon their having been reduced to abject submission. He was not to be frightened by their threats, however, now that he was in the open air with the redcoated soldiery all around him; and instead of obeying Nathan's command he brandished his fists as he cried:

"Get back to the house until I can learn what is to be done with you."

"We will give you the information without any necessity for your returning," Evan said with a laugh, which only served to irritate the Tory. "We have Major Ferguson's permission to depart, and count on doing so without allowing ourselves to be delayed by such as you."

"Major Ferguson's permission to depart!" Ephraim repeated stupidly.

"Step aside, or we may be called upon to put you out of our path with more force than is agreeable."

"You lie when you say the major has released you!"

"Hark you, Ephraim Sowers; I am not minded to get into a brawl hereabouts; but so much as repeat that word, and I shall give no heed as to the consequences," Nathan said sternly. "You and I have a long reckoning to be settled, and I do not desire to begin it now; yet I shall if you are not choice of your words."

Ephraim looked from one to the other questioningly, as if trying to decide how he might best reduce these lads to the proper state of submission, and then called peremptorily to a soldier who was passing near by:

"Hello there! Here are two prisoners who count on escaping by pretending that Major Ferguson has given them permission to depart. Come and take them in charge."

"Are these your orders, or do you repeat some other's words?"

"Don't stop to talk; but lay hold of these two rebels, lest by sheer boldness they succeed in making off."

"Best keep a quiet and civil tongue in your head, youngster, for I am not minded to take orders from one who does such dirty work as you," the soldier said surlily, and passed on, leaving Ephraim crimson with rage.

Near by where the boys had been halted was a stack of muskets, and running quickly up to them the Tory seized one, regardless of the fact that by so doing he allowed all the others to fall to the ground.

Then, turning suddenly, he aimed the weapon full at the two lads, crying as he did so:

"Wheel about, and march back to the house, or I shall shoot. Don't think you can get the upperhand of me as readily as you did last night, for I am not minded to deal gently with you now."

"Ho, there! Guard!" a voice cried. "Seize that lad and let him be deprived of his liberty until he has sense enough to keep in his own station."

The soldier who had refused to obey Ephraim wheeled about suddenly upon receiving this command from Captain Depuyster, who had just come from the dwelling, and before the young Tory was well aware of the change in the position of affairs, he was being marched toward the stables, the trooper's hand clutching his collar so tightly as to render breathing a difficult operation.

"You can go on now, and see to it that you do not loiter, until you have repeated Major Ferguson's words to the rebels round about."

Once more the boys set their faces toward Greene's Spring, and as they marched rapidly away the captain followed them until they were past the line of sentinels.

Then he turned on his heel, and the two who had so lately been prisoners slackened not their pace until a mile or more was traversed, when as if with one accord they came to a halt, in order to congratulate each other upon the fortunate and unexpected turn of affairs.

It is not necessary to repeat here what they said, for one can well fancy how extravagant were their words and demonstrations of joy at finding themselves free when it had seemed positive they were doomed to a long term of imprisonment, during which time Ephraim Sowers might often play the part of jailer.

They hugged each other as if the thankfulness in their hearts could be thus shown better than by words, and laughed loud and long at the discomfiture of the Tory spy, who had counted so certainly on making them atone for their treatment of him.

In fact, so elated were the lads that their words as well as gestures were extravagant; perhaps half an hour had thus been spent before either bethought himself that it was necessary they should push ahead with all speed, for no rations had been served since the night previous, and food was not to be obtained until they were among friends once more.

Once the boys were well on the journey, and after the first excess of joy had passed away, both realized their extreme weariness.

The previous day was spent in marching. No sleep had come during the night, and much excitement had tended to increase their fatigue.

Now twenty miles must be traversed, without food, before they could gain the needed rest, and it is not strange that when another hour passed they found it difficult to continue the advance.

More than once Evan urged that a halt be made for two or three hours, lest they should not be able to hold out until the end; but Nathan steadily refused to listen to any suggestions, and they toiled painfully on, stumbling here or staggering there, hardly conscious of their movements.

It was as if in a dream that they finally saw that band of Americans who had repulsed the British forces a few hours previous, and then all was a blank, for consciousness literally deserted them.

During the remainder of the day and all of the following night the weary lads slept.

The sun was rising, and Colonel Clarke's men were making ready for a change of camp, when Captain Dillard awakened the lads by shaking each gently by the arm, as he cried in a cheery tone:

"Rise up, or sleep will wear your eyes out. Unless I am much mistaken you are more in need of food just now than of additional slumber, and it is time you were stirring."

The boys sprang to their feet refreshed by the long repose, and ravenously hungry, but so eager were they to learn the particulars of the combat which they had heard from the distance that neither realized his need of food.

"You shall hear it all very shortly; but it will be on full stomachs, for I am not minded to have you starve yet awhile, and it is Sarah's right to tell the story."

"Then Mrs. Dillard did get here in time?" Nathan cried.

"Ay, lads, else were we like to have been murdered while we slept. And a brave ride it was; but I am not the one to tell it. Come over by the fire, and after you have filled yourselves up I will put you in the way to listen to all which I know you are eager to hear."

Half an hour later, after they had literally obeyed the injunction to "fill themselves up," the boys and Captain Dillard were pressing on in advance of the American force, to the dwelling where Mrs. Dillard had sought shelter, and before noon they had arrived at their destination.

There was much to be told on both sides, and as the quickest method of gaining the information he desired, Nathan first explained how they had left the British camp, and gave all the details of their advance from the time of parting with Mrs. Dillard on the mountain trail.

Then it was his turn to act the part of listener, and eagerly did he and Evan drink in the vivid account of that night ride, and the combat which ensued.

It seemed as if the colt recognized the uselessness of struggling further against the determined woman who was bent on riding him, for when the boys had let go their hold he darted forward straight as an arrow over the trail, and at full speed.

There were many places where the narrow road ran along the side of the mountain, when a single misstep would have thrown him headlong over the cliffs, and yet no mountaineer's steed ever traveled with a surer footing, and at so swift a pace.

Once only did he make any effort at throwing his rider. Then, fortunately, it was in a valley where there were no trees, and Sarah Dillard was sufficiently expert an equestrienne to baffle him.

During ten minutes or more the steed plunged and kicked, and then, as if again becoming convinced that he must carry the life-saving message, he darted onward, slackening not the pace until they were arrived in the midst of the encampment.

The amazement of the patriots at seeing the hostess from whom they had so lately parted at such an hour, can well be fancied, and it may also be readily understood that, having accomplished the dangerous journey, Sarah Dillard lost no time in making known the fateful news which she brought.

One word was sufficient to these men who were inured to hardships of every kind and accustomed to face danger in every form.

Within five minutes after Mrs. Dillard's arrival they were prepared to give Major Ferguson's force a warm reception, and so sure were the men in their ability to hold the encampment against the enemy, that a squad of four was sent, as escort to the brave rider, a dozen miles or more away where dwelt one in whose fidelity to the Cause there could be no question.

The colt, so Captain Dillard said, had done his share in saving the lives of an hundred men, and he should be called upon to perform no meaner work so long as he might live, than that of bearing on his back the woman who had literally taken her life in her hands when she set out on that perilous ride.

As to the combat, the captain dismissed it with few words:

"We were ready for the redcoats when they came up, and had been for two hours or more. When the horses were picketed our scouts brought us word, and then it was only a question of figuring in our own minds how long it would take them to creep up on us.

"We could see the Britishers as they surrounded the encampment; but never a man raised his gun until they had their muskets at their shoulders, and then we sent a volley among them that mowed down a full half of those in the front rank. I thought at the moment that they would retreat without so much as firing a shot, because of the astonishment which must have come over them.

"There is no doubt of that," the other soldier replied, and straightway the men began making the horses ready for departure, as if they expected their comrades would come back in full flight, and need the means of continuing it.

When five minutes more had passed there was no longer any question as to the result of the combat.

By this time the British were so near where the horses had been left that now and then stray bullets whistled among the branches above the heads of the prisoners, and the two lads began debating how it might be possible for them to escape when the troop should be in full flight.

However kind Fortune had been to the Americans on this night, she was not so indulgent as to give the lads their liberty.

As could be told from the rattle of musketry, the British made a stand after fifteen minutes' or more of hot fighting, and the Americans, having accomplished as much, and, perhaps, even more than they had expected, were willing the invaders should draw off if such was their disposition.

In less than half an hour from the time they set out to massacre the supposedly sleeping encampment, the redcoats had returned, and, standing by their horses, awaiting the command to mount. Now it was that even in the gloom the boys could see how many of the animals were without riders.

There had been no empty saddles when the troop rode up, and now on looking around there was hardly a squad of horses where more than two out of five had a man standing by his side.

"The slaughter was not wholly among our friends," Evan whispered to Nathan, and the latter, bent only on trying to escape, said hurriedly:

"Think of nothing but yourself just now. There must be a chance for us to give them the slip amid all this confusion."

He had no more than spoken before one of the officers came up and asked of those standing near by:

"Who had charge of these lads?"

The two troopers who had made the capture replied to the question, and then came the order:

"See to it that you hold them fast. There is no reason why your own beasts should carry double while there are so many spare horses; but lash them firmly to the saddles, for Major Ferguson must have speech with them by daylight."

By some means the patriots had been warned in due season, and were ready to meet the foe, as they ever had been.

"It is Sarah Dillard's ride that has saved them!" Evan exclaimed as if questioning the truth of his own statement, and straightway Nathan fell to weeping, so great was the relief which came upon him as he realized that the friends of freedom had been prepared for the foe.

The troopers nearabout the boys were so excited and astonished, because what they had counted on as being a complete surprise proved to have been a failure, that no one heard Evan's remark, and the prisoners could have shouted for very joy when the men began speculating one with the other as to how word might have been sent to the patriots.

"It is certain they were ready to receive us," one man said as if in anger because the plan was miscarrying. "That firing is being done by men who were ready for battle as were ours. There has been a traitor in the camp."

"How might that be?" another asked fiercely. "At the last halting-place we were twenty miles from the rebel encampment, and certain it is no one could have ridden ahead of us."

"These two boy did succeed in escaping, despite the fact that Major Ferguson believed them to be safe in the chamber of the dwelling."

"Ay; but what does that prove? We overtook them on the way, and surely you cannot claim that they might have walked twenty miles from the time of escaping until they were recaptured?"

The rattle of musketry increased, and to the eager ears of the boys it seemed as if the noise of the conflict was approaching, which would indicate that the Britishers were being driven back.

"Does it appear to you as if we heard those sounds more clearly?" Nathan asked, hoping he had not been mistaken, and yet feeling almost certain the patriots could do but little more than hold their own.

"I am positive of it!" Evan cried with a ring of joy and triumph in his tone. "Now and then I can hear voices even amid the tumult, and that was impossible five minutes ago."

One of the troopers, overhearing this remark, said to his comrade gloomily:

"The rebels are getting the best of us, who counted on taking them completely by surprise."

perhaps never were two lads shown more respect than they, because of the fact that they were doing, and had done, the work of men, although only boys.

They were justly proud on the day of their arrival at Watuga, to be received by these sturdy patriots like equals, and to be besieged on every side with questions as to the general feeling among the people of the districts which they had visited.

Evan's father gave them a place in his troop, and when some of the men insisted that the boys should be allowed to play the part of officers because of the particular and difficult work they had performed, Colonel McDowells replied:

"If it is the purpose of the lads to serve their country, they can best do so with muskets in their hands, but if they simply desire to parade themselves before the people in fine feathers, the Carolinas is no place for them. They had better go where they can have better fare and more opportunity for admiration."

It troubled the boys but little that, after having been intrusted with important business, they were to have no more responsible part than that of private soldiers, for they knew full well that neither was fitted for a command, and it sufficed that the privilege was given them to serve the cause in howsoever humble capacity.

They were in the ranks on that th day of September when the little force went out from Watuga down the Catawba River, and by the th of October, when the patriots had arrived at the Cowpens where Colonel Williams kept his word by marching up with twenty men more than he had promised, it was said among the men as well as the officers that there were no more promising soldiers in the force than these two lads whose first experience in military matters had been gained as prisoners.

During this time they made diligent inquiries of all who might have such information concerning Ephraim Sowers, but without learning anything whatsoever.

"Don't let that fret you, lads," Captain Dillard said when they went into camp at the Cowpens, and learned from the scouts that Major Ferguson's force was encamped not more than thirty miles distant near the Cherokee Ford of Broad River. "Don't let that fret you. Unless I am very much mistaken, we shall not remain here many hours, for there is a council of war being held, and from what I know of our commanding officers, we shall give the gallant major all the hot work he can desire. Then, if your Tory spy be not weak-kneed, you will have an opportunity of coming face to face with him, for once we have met this gentleman who proposes to lay waste our country with fire and sword, we shall not leave him until after having made the acquaintance of a goodly number of his men."

"But Ephraim Sowers is not a soldier," Evan said with a laugh, "and I am of the opinion that he is weak-kneed."

"Even then the chances are he yet remains with Ferguson's troop, for hark you, lad, the Tories have joined the major in such numbers that hereabouts in the Carolinas are none left at their homes. The spy must stick to his red-coated friends whom he served so well, or have a mighty lonesome time of it by himself. If I had played his part, doing all in my power to bring about the death of those who had befriended me, I should make it my business to keep ever within sight of a red uniform, lest some of those whose death I had sought to compass might fall upon me. You shall see Ephraim Sowers and have a long talk with him."

"You speak, Captain, as if there could be no question of the result, once we are come up with the force."

"Neither is there, lad. We of the Carolinas have each a home to protect, and so many wrongs to avenge that there can be no backward move on our part once the fight is opened."

"How many men think you Major Ferguson can muster?"

"In regulars and Tories from fourteen to fifteen hundred."

"And our own forces?"

"Not far from seventeen hundred."

"Then we are the stronger?"

"Not so, Nathan, my boy. Did we number two thousand the force would hardly be equal, because of disparity of weapons. The king's troops are well equipped, and they bring with them muskets and ammunition in plenty for the Tories who join them. We have only such as each man can provide, and some of us so poorly armed that half a dozen rounds would see the powder-horns and shot pouches emptied. But we are fighting for the cause, and they for the King. In that you have the whole story, and therefore this I say: When we come face to face with Major Ferguson, as I believe we shall within twenty-four hours, we will stay with him so long that you will have ample time in which to seek out this spy who would have compassed the death of us at Greene's Spring."

CHAPTER VIII.

THE PRISONER.

Nathan and Evan were enjoying to the utmost this conversation with Captain Dillard.

It is true they had seen him seldom since the first greeting after Sarah Dillard's ride; but on each occasion he had appeared much as if trying to show the world that he had espoused respect and admiration for these two lads.

This was particularly pleasing to the boys, because Captain Dillard was one who was choice of his associates, and it was often said that "Dillard's friendship was given only to brave men."

Nathan and Evan were proud at being seen with this gallant Carolinian as if they were his bosom friends, and when a messenger came from Colonel McDowells summoning them to an interview with the commander of the forces from Burke and Rutherford, they were not well pleased at being obliged to part company from the man who among all the troops they most admired.

With evident reluctance they rose to their feet, and while walking toward Colonel McDowells' quarters, Nathan said:

"I don't think we did any very gallant deed, Evan, when we turned the tables on Ephraim Sowers, or aided Sarah Dillard to remount the colt. Neither have we done anything of which to boast in repeating Major Ferguson's message, or summoning friends of the cause to the rendezvous; but yet because of all those adventures have we been marked out before the entire camp as lads with whom Captain Dillard is pleased to hold conversation, and even though we had suffered much, such a reward would be sufficient."

"The captain believes we shall come up with the Britishers within twenty-four hours," Evan said, as if he had not heard his comrade's remark.

"Ay, and it is said they are only twenty miles away, eager to meet us."

"Then there is like to be battle."

"Ay; how else could it be when both sides are ready to fight?"

"And shall you rejoice at finding yourself standing musket in hand before the foe?"

"Of a verity I shall! Why not? Would you avoid the encounter if it could be done honorably?" and halting suddenly, Nathan looked his comrade full in the face.

"It is a shameful thing for a lad to say, of that I am well aware," Evan replied hesitatingly; "but I grow timorous at the thought, and have great fear lest I shall betray some signs of cowardice."

Nathan laughed long and loud.

"When Captain Charles McDowells' son, he whose grandmother has proven herself on more than one occasion to be as brave as the most courageous men, speaks of showing cowardice, there is reason for laughing."

"But I have never stood in line with soldiers during the heat of battle, and fear much lest I should shame my father."

"You never have done so yet, lad, and I will answer for it that he has no cause to blush in your behalf. Put such idle fancies from your mind, and when the hour comes that we meet Major Ferguson's force, never fear but that you will be foremost among the friends of freedom."

Evan would have said more regarding this sudden timorousness which had come upon him, but for the fact that they were then arrived at Colonel McDowells' tent, and the subject of the interview for which he had summoned them was so startling and unexpected as to drive all other thoughts from the boy's mind.

"You two, who claim the right to be called soldiers, although never having marched in the ranks until the day we left Watuga, know full well that the Britishers are within thirty or forty miles of us at this moment."

The colonel paused as if for reply, and Evan said:

"We have heard it so spoken among the men, sir."

"You understand, also, that we are like to measure strength with them before many hours?"

"Yes, sir."

"While I cast no discredit on your courage, I am free to say that men who have had more experience in this business will be of greater service to us in time of battle than you lads."

"But surely, father, you won't say that we shall not bear our share in the combat," Evan cried, suddenly forgetting the fears of which he had made mention to his comrade.

"It is not my purpose to prevent you from bearing your full share of danger, and in fact I now propose to place you in a position more perilous than, perhaps, would be your regular stations in the regiment. I simply wish to explain why I called upon you for a certain service, rather than men who may be needed elsewhere."

The boys looked in bewilderment at the colonel, trying in vain to understand the meaning of this vague explanation, and after a brief pause he continued:

"It has been proposed that we send out a certain number of men to gain all possible information regarding the strength and disposition of the enemy. To such suggestions I have argued that we could ill afford to spare even two soldiers, and yet I know it is necessary we should have such knowledge. Therefore have I said to those who are associated with me in the command, that we would hold those who had already proven themselves, and send out such as yet had a name to win. The mission is one of extreme danger, and requires most careful work. If you lads shrink not from the task, I would have you volunteer to set about it, for this is a service to which I would not order any person. Go, if you can, of your own free will; but if the undertaking seems too dangerous, no one shall taunt you for having refused."

"Where are we to go, sir?" Evan asked.

"As near to Major Ferguson's encampment as may be necessary in order to learn exactly the number and disposition of his men."

"When are we to start?"

"As soon as may be. There is no time for delay, since we must push forward steadily, and not allow it to be believed that we shrink from the battle."

"Then it would be best Evan and I did not spend any further time in asking questions," Nathan interrupted. "We will be off at once."

"And you have no hesitation about the matter, young Shelby?" Colonel McDowells asked as he gazed at the boys sharply.

"Both Evan and I are ready to do all that may be in our power, and even though the task was one which we shrank from, both of us have too much pride to allow that fact to become known. However, this doesn't seem as dangerous as when we set out about making our escape from the Dillard plantation, and there is no reason why we should falter. My only fear is lest we may not be sufficiently well versed in military matters to bring such information as is required."

"Keep your eyes and ears open, remembering everything which is seen and heard, and I doubt not but that you can perform the mission as well as the ablest soldier among us. It is necessary you exercise great prudence, however, for should Major Ferguson detect you in loitering around his encampment, he would be justified in hanging you as spies with but scant ceremony."

"Have you any further orders, sir?" Evan asked nervously, for this reminder of the peril they were about to incur was not pleasing.

"None," and the colonel rose to his feet as he held out both hands to the boys.

A fervent hand-clasp was the only token of parting, and the lads went directly from this interview to prepare themselves for the journey.

Captain Dillard came up as they were refilling the powder horns, and counting out an additional store of bullets.

"So the colonel has sent his son rather than risk the life of one of the men," he said half to himself, and Evan looked up with a smile as he replied:

"When favors are to be bestowed, captain, it is right the father should remember first his son."

"And this is a favor with a vengeance," Dillard muttered, after which, realizing he had been imprudent in thus voicing his apprehensions, he whistled a cheery tune as if there was no reason why he or any other in the encampment should be gloomy.

In less than ten minutes the boys had made their preparations for the scout, and were debating as to the best course to be pursued.

"Make straight for Cherokee Ford, lads, and trust to luck for all the remainder. I do not mean that you are to go blindly ahead without taking due precautions; but it seldom pays at such times to map out an elaborate plan, for much depends upon accident."

Then the captain turned abruptly away, most likely to avoid a leave-taking, and the two boys marched side by side out of the encampment, the men following them with their eyes but speaking no word, for each understood upon what a perilous venture they were embarked.

It was nightfall, and the young scouts were unfamiliar with the country over which it would be necessary to travel.

They knew, however, that a well-defined trail led from the Cowpens to Cherokee Ford, and along this they advanced at a smart pace, for it seemed necessary the journey should be performed during the hours of darkness.

Neither felt inclined for conversation. The silence of the men as they left the encampment struck them much like predictions of evil, and they were weighted down by a sense of danger in the air everywhere around them.

At near midnight they made the first halt, and up to that time not more than half a dozen words had been exchanged.

Now it was as if the nearness of the foe revived their courage rather than depressed them, and they discussed the situation as calmly as they might have spoken of the most ordinary affair.

"We must have been five hours on the march, and covered no less than seventeen or eighteen miles," Nathan suggested.

"Surely we are that far from the encampment, and it stands us in hand to have an eye out for redcoats, because they or the Tories will likely be scouting nearabout their halting place."

"And by going blindly ahead we may come upon them sooner than would be pleasant," Nathan added with a laugh. "Now it is my proposition that we tarry here until daybreak, rather than run our noses into trouble."

"Father said we were to perform the mission as quickly as might be."

"True; but yet he did not propose that we discover the foe by running into their very midst."

"We are yet a good dozen miles from Cherokee Ford, and by waiting here until daybreak will be forced to spend three or four hours before we can hope to see the main body."

"If it is your belief that we should push on yet further, I am ready," Nathan replied in a tone of content, and thus it was decided that they should not make camp until having arrived at least six miles nearer the supposed location of the Britishers.

After fifteen minutes had been spent in resting the lads set forward again, and, as nearly as they could judge, it was two o'clock in the morning when Evan announced that he was ready to make a lengthy halt.

Creeping into the thicket a few yards from the trail where they could remain concealed from view, and yet be enabled to see any who might pass, the boys set about gaining such repose as might be possible.

One slept while the other watched, and every half-hour they changed positions, so that by daybreak each had had his share of slumber.

When the first grey light of dawn appeared they set out for the final and most perilous stage of the journey, advancing cautiously, halting to listen at every unfamiliar sound, and oftentimes making a detour through the thicket when there was a sharp bend in the trail which might have led them suddenly upon a scouting party of the foe.

By such method their progress was exceedingly slow, and by sunrise they had advanced no more than three miles.

Now if the information brought to the American encampment was correct, they were close upon the Britishers, and might at any moment expect to see a scarlet coat through the foliage.

"We must take some chances in order to push ahead more rapidly, or we shall not be able to return before to-morrow morning," Nathan whispered impatiently, after they had literally crawled through the thicket half an hour more, and the words were hardly uttered when the sounds of footsteps upon the beaten path a short distance in advance of them, caused both to suddenly seek a hiding-place.

It is well the lads were on the alert, for within a few seconds four Britishers came down the trail in a leisurely fashion, as if out for no other purpose than that of a stroll, and Evan gripped Nathan's arm hard as he saw in the rear of these men none other than Ephraim Sowers.

The young Tory was walking slowly, as if displeased with himself for having ventured away from the camp, while the Britishers were in the best of spirits, laughing and chatting merrily without paying any attention to their gloomy-visaged companion.

It was when he arrived at a point directly opposite the hidden scouts that Ephraim stopped, leaned his musket against a rock, and seated himself upon a fallen tree-trunk, as he said petulantly:

"I am tired of this wandering around when we are like to come upon a party of rebels at any minute."

"Then why do you follow? No person prevents you from returning to the camp," one of the soldiers said with a laugh.

"I am minded to go back alone, and you know full well the orders were that no man should stray very far from the mountain."

"Then you are not disobeying, since I'll go bail there's little of the man about you."

"How dare you speak in that way when Major Ferguson is nearby to overhear the words?" and now Ephraim displayed anger.

"Don't pride yourself, lad, on being the especial pet of the major. He is not given to much affection for cowards, even though they be spies, and I am willing to wager considerable that no member of the command would be reproved for speaking harshly to such as you."

During this brief conversation the soldiers had continued to advance, while Ephraim remained sitting upon the log, and when the last remark was made the redcoats were hidden from view by the foliage.

The young Tory kicked idly at the earth in front of him, looked up and down the trail as if in search of something entertaining, and then leaned lazily back against a convenient bush.

The footsteps of the soldiers sounded fainter and fainter in the distance, telling that the men were continuing to advance, until finally all was silent.

The two lads were within forty feet of the boy who would have done the cause of freedom such grievous wrong, and each instant those who might lend him a helping hand were drawing further away.

Nathan glanced at Evan with a question in his eye, and the latter understood it as well as if he had spoken.

"It might be done," he whispered cautiously; "but we should not neglect the work which was set us."

"It is not safe to advance while these men are between us and Major Ferguson's force, therefore unless we make him prisoner it is necessary to remain idle."

"What could be done with him?"

"I'll venture to say he might be frightened into telling all we would know."

Nathan hesitated an instant. They had been sent out solely to gain some knowledge of the enemy's force and disposition. To take this boy a prisoner, even though he was their bitterest foe, seemed to be deviating from the course Colonel McDowells had marked out, but yet, as Nathan said, they must remain idle there until these four men should return. Therefore it would not be such a woeful waste of time.

"If we can do it without giving the alarm, I am ready," Evan whispered, and instead of replying, Nathan began creeping cautiously in the direction of the Tory, who sat with his back turned toward them.

Many a time had these two lads crept quietly upon a flock of wild turkeys without alarming the shy birds, and to go through the same maneuvers when a dull boy like Ephraim Sowers was the game to be stalked did not prove difficult.

Side by side they advanced with hardly so much as disturbing a single twig, and had gained the cover of a bush within three feet of him before he so much as changed his position.

Then he started to his feet, and the two in hiding crouched yet closer to the ground, fearing lest he had grown suspicious; but it was merely to change his position, and after looking up and down the trail, muttering threats against the soldiers because they continued their stroll when it was not to his liking, he reseated himself without having so much as touched his musket.

It was possible the redcoats might even now be retracing their steps, and whatever the lads counted on doing must be done without loss of time.

Nathan pressed Evan's hand in token that he was ready for the venture, and the latter nodded his head.

The two rose to their feet, standing motionless a single instant, and then, darting forward with a sudden spring, they landed directly upon the unsuspecting Tory.

Nathan had counted upon covering the spy's mouth with his hand; but missed the aim, and Ephraim was enabled to utter one shrill cry, after which he was powerless to do more than breathe.

"Work quickly now, for the soldiers may have heard that, and we are like to be prisoners ourselves instead of capturing this sneak," Nathan whispered. "We must tie his hands again, and contrive something for a gag quickly."

As deftly, and yet more rapidly than on that night when Sarah Dillard rode the unbroken colt, Evan bound the prisoner, and from the time they first leaped upon him until Ephraim's hands were tied and his mouth choked by a portion of his own garments, no more than three minutes had passed.

"Take his musket, for it must appear as if he had gone back to the camp, and see to it that you wipe out all traces of a struggle, while I carry him into the thicket."

Then the boy lifted Ephraim to his shoulder as if he had been no more than a package of bulky merchandise, and while Evan carried out the instructions to the best of his ability, the spy was taken an hundred yards or more into the thicket.

Here Nathan halted until his comrade joined him, when the two continued the flight until they were fully half a mile from the trail, and all this while Ephraim Sowers was unable to give vent to his anger or his fears.

"That was a neat job, and one that need not interfere with the purpose of our journey," Nathan said in a tone of exultation, as he wiped the perspiration from his face and sat down where he could look full at the discomfited Tory. "By this means we have made certain of coming face to face with Ephraim Sowers again, for I misdoubt if he would have been found in the battle unless peradventure the Britishers were getting much the best of it."

"Now that we have got the sneak, what is to be done with him?"

"Tie him up here until we have concluded our work, and then carry him back to the men of Colonel Clarke's command, who have a score to settle because of his efforts to deliver them over to their butchers."

The expression in Ephraim's eyes gave good token of the terror which was in his heart, and in furtherance of the plan he had lately conceived Nathan took the gag from the boy's mouth.

"Those men would murder me!" Ephraim screamed as soon as his mouth was freed from the gag.

"Ay, so it appears to me, else will they be more forgiving than I can well believe," Nathan replied calmly, as if in his mind the spy was already doomed.

"Would you take me, who has never done you any wrong, to where I shall be killed?" he whined.

"How much wrong would you have done had we not set upon you the night the force at Greene's Spring were to be massacred?" Evan asked sternly. "When we were again captured was it in your mind to treat us as friends?"

"I would not have killed you."

"Then you lied in order to frighten us."

"I did want to make you weaken, but had no thought of doing you a wrong."

"Such a controversy is useless, and we have not the time to spend upon it," Nathan interrupted. "Colonel Clarke's men are doubtless eager to meet with this Tory who devoted so much of his time to them, and if it so be we are forced to continue on in order to gain information concerning the Britishers, we can do no other than deliver him up to them."

"What is it you want to know?" Ephraim asked, a ray of hope coming into his eyes.

"We are sent to learn concerning the British forces. How many there are, where they are encamped, and such other matters as may be necessary for the guidance of those who direct the attack."

"Is there to be a battle?" Ephraim asked eagerly.

"Not before we have had time to deliver you over to those who will thank us for so doing."

The gleam of hope died away very suddenly, and the spy, knowing full well what would likely be his fate, did he fall into the hands of the men who would have been killed or captured had his plans not failed, now gave evidence of the liveliest terror.

"If you will save my life, I swear to tell you all I know about Major Ferguson's forces, and none can give the information better, for I have been with them every hour since you were allowed to leave Dillard's plantation."

"It might be that we could take advantage of the offer, if it was possible to believe a single word you uttered," Nathan said, as if debating whether to accept the proposition or not.

"I swear to you that every word shall be true, and if you hold me prisoner it will be easy to know whether I have told the truth or not," Ephraim pleaded. "Promise that if I give all the information needed you will save my life, and you shall have such a description of the camp as could not be gotten by scouting around it for a week."

"Shall we accept the offer, Evan?" Nathan asked, as if it was a matter of indifference to him, and Ephraim cried imploringly:

"Give me one chance! Don't turn me over to those who have good reason for murdering me! I will answer every question truly, and you shall keep me prisoner until it has been proven that all I said was correct."

CHAPTER IX.

KING'S MOUNTAIN.

Having brought Ephraim Sowers into that frame of mind where he could be utilized, Nathan made the pretense of consulting with Evan as to the advisability of accepting the spy's information.

"If Evan will agree to it, we may promise that you shall not be given up to Colonel Clarke's men, although, as a matter of course, we have no intention of setting you at liberty."

"All I ask is that you put me under the charge of Colonel Charles McDowells, you promising me in his name that I shall receive the same treatment as any other prisoner."

"It is a great deal you are asking, Ephraim Sowers, after all you have done and tried to do; but it may be that we can arrange it. Come this way, Evan," and Nathan stepped aside a few paces to give the Tory an idea that considerable argument would be necessary in order to induce his comrade to enter into the agreement.

"Can we believe what he says?" Evan asked when he and Nathan stood at such a distance from the prisoner that their words could not be overheard.

"I do not understand how he would dare to tell a lie. When our men advance it will be known if he has given the correct information, and we will make it plain that should he tell us anything which was proven to be incorrect, then our promises are withdrawn."

"Go on, and arrange the matter as soon as you can, for no one can say when some of the redcoats may come this way on a scout, and if we should chance to fall into the hands of the enemy now, I think that Tory sneak would kill us, if the murder could be compassed."

The two remained as if in conversation a moment longer, and then returning to the terrified spy, Nathan said in a solemn tone:

"We have agreed that if you give us all the information in your power concerning Major Ferguson's force, and you claim to know everything regarding it, we will carry you as prisoner to Evan's father, promising in his name that you shall be treated the same as any Britisher that might be captured. Should, however, it be discovered that you played us false in the slightest detail, it will be the same as if our promise had not been given, and you will be turned over to Colonel Clarke's men."

"I am not likely to tell that which is not true when my life depends upon the truth," Ephraim said in a tone which convinced his hearers that, perhaps for the first time in his life, he was resolved to make a correct statement.

"Well," Evan said impatiently after a brief pause. "Why don't you begin?"

"What shall I tell you?"

"How many men has Major Ferguson?"

"I must not be held as to the truth of numbers, for I only know what I heard a commissary sergeant say, which was that there were eleven hundred and twenty all told upon the mountain."

"What mountain?"

"The force is encamped on the summit of King's Mountain, which is about twelve miles north of the Cherokee Ford."

"How far from here?"

"I should say less than an hour's march."

"Have the troops any other weapons than muskets?"

"No."

"How many are the king's soldiers, and how many Tories?"

"There are not above two hundred of his majesty's troops."

"Have you any idea why the major chanced to take that place as an encampment?"

"Our scouts have brought in the word that the rebels were gathering in large numbers, and the major established his camp where it could not well be attacked."

"How long has he been there?"

"Two days."

"Do you know if he intends making a move soon?"

"I have heard it said in the camp that we were like to stay there a long while— at least until reinforcements can be sent by General Cornwallis."

"Beside the men who came out with you on the trail, how many are scouting around in this neighborhood?"

"There are perhaps twenty who set out this morning."

"Are they soldiers or Tories?"

"I suppose you would call them Tories, but nevertheless they are royalists."

"There is a distinction without a difference in those terms, Ephraim," Nathan said grimly, "but I'll venture to say there are very few who are both Tory and spy, with an inclination to bring death upon those who had befriended them."

"In taking to Major Ferguson information as to Colonel Clarke's force I only did my duty, for I was serving the king, and should look upon all those who offer armed resistance to his laws as enemies."

"You were not so strict in your allegiance last winter, when you begged for food."

Ephraim winced but made no reply, and Evan said thoughtfully:

"It appears to me we have gotten all the information he has to give, and it stands us in hand to return to camp as soon as may be, if you think we are justified in pinning our faith upon his statements."

"I swear that I have told you only the truth," Ephraim cried, beginning to fear lest his captors might recede from the position they had taken.

"If there are twenty Britishers scouting around the mountain I do not believe we can learn any more than he has told us," Nathan said half to himself, "and it appears to me as if we had good reason for believing our mission had been fulfilled."

"Then let us lose no time in retracing our steps, for there yet remains twenty-six or twenty-seven miles to be traversed nightfall."

"Where are your forces encamped?" Ephraim asked.

"At the Cowpens, on Broad River. I heard Captain Depuyster say, when it was told him that some of the rebels—I mean your friends—were gathered there, that it was twenty-eight miles away."

"Then you know the exact distance it is necessary for you to walk before sunset," Nathan replied. "We shall not be so cruel as to confine your arms, but you must march not more than three paces in advance of us, and remember, Ephraim Sowers, if you make any movement which has the appearance as if you were trying to give us the slip, we shall fire with intent to kill, and at such short range there can be little doubt as to the accuracy of our aim. Are you ready, Evan?"

"Yes, and the sooner we set out the better I shall be pleased."

But for the fact that the young Tory was dependent upon these two for his life, he would have remonstrated against being forced to make so long and hurried a journey; but under the circumstances he did not dare say a single word which might sound like a complaint.

He waited meekly until Nathan pointed out the direction to be pursued, and then set off as if eager to arrive at the destination, his captors meanwhile keeping their eyes upon him and being on the alert for any attempt at escape.

There is little to tell regarding this long tramp, a portion of which was made through the thicket, and the remainder over the trail, save to say that both the prisoner and his captors were nearly exhausted before it came to an ending.

Twice only did they halt, and then not more than ten minutes at a time, lest by remaining quiet too long their wearied limbs should become stiffened.

Evan and Nathan had brought with them a scanty supply of food, and this they shared with Ephraim; but it was so small in quantity that it served hardly more than to whet their appetites, and when, shortly after sunset, they were arrived at the American encampment, it seemed to all three as if they were literally on the verge of exhaustion.

The coming of the boys was hailed with shouts of joy by the men, and when it was learned who they brought with them as prisoner, it appeared much as if the promise Ephraim's captors had made would avail him nothing.

Before they could make their way to Colonel McDowells' quarters the three were surrounded by a throng of hungry men, who insisted that the Tory should be hanged offhand for his crime; and but little attention was paid to the entreaties of Nathan and Evan, who announced again and again that they had pledged their word for his safety.

"We have sworn that he shall be put into the custody of Colonel Charles McDowells, and trusting in our word he has given us valuable information concerning the enemy," Nathan cried at the full strength of his lungs, when the throng became so great that they were forced to come to a halt.

"Hang the spy! He is one who brought Ferguson's troopers down to Greene's Spring that Clarke's men might be massacred. Hang him!"

Ephraim kneeled upon the ground, clinging to the legs of the boys, alternately praying that they would guard him and reminding them of the promises made.

"Although he merits death we will keep faith with him, and he who lays a hand on the Tory must first dispose of us!" Evan cried.

The men were in no mood to listen to reason, and it is more than likely the boys would have failed in their purpose but that Colonel William Campbell, hearing the tumult, came quickly up to learn the cause.

Hurriedly and in the fewest possible words Nathan explained the situation of affairs, and Ephraim's life was saved for the time being, for the colonel, calling for the Virginia force, formed a guard around the prisoner and his captors, holding the mob in check until all were arrived at Colonel McDowells' quarters.

Here Ephraim was delivered to Evan's father and Colonel James Williams, and these two officers decided that the young scouts had acted wisely in returning, for they placed every dependence in the statements made by Ephraim, who, as Colonel Williams said, "had for the first time the truth frightened out of him."

The lads were directed to go in search of food, and when, an hour later, they returned to Colonel McDowells' quarters, Ephraim was nowhere to be seen.

"What have you done with the Tory?" Evan asked, fearing for the instant lest his father had forgotten that their word was pledged for his safe keeping.

"It was best he should not remain in camp, for the men were grown so excited that I doubt if I could have held them in check. Your spy has been sent away where we can make certain he will be held in safe custody."

Then the colonel asked for the details of the journey just ended, and when this had been given, he startled them by saying:

"Since receiving the information from Ephraim Sowers, it has been decided that we will set out at once in pursuit of the enemy, lest Major Ferguson change his plans, and lead us a long chase. We have nine hundred men well mounted, and these will start within an hour, continuing the march until they shall come up with the enemy; meanwhile the footmen, and those whose animals are not in the best of condition, will follow as fast as possible."

"Do you intend to attack the Britishers, intrenched as they are on the mountain?" Evan asked in surprise.

"Ay, lad, we will set upon them wherever they may be found, and whip them too, till there shall be no more left of this force which has come to lay waste the country with fire and sword."

"But what of Nathan and I?" Evan asked anxiously. "Are we to be left behind?"

"It is time you had some rest, lads, and better you should follow with those who march afoot."

"In that case, sir, we might miss the battle," Nathan interrupted.

"Perhaps it were better if you did."

"We have thought, sir, Evan and I, that because of working hard for the cause, we would be given the first opportunity to show what we might do."

"And you are eager to go into the combat?" Colonel McDowells asked of his son.

"It would sadden me if I was not allowed to do so, sir, although, as I have confessed to Nathan several times, I fear my courage may fail me."

"If it does, you will be the first McDowells who has shown the white feather, and perhaps it is time we should know whether you are of the right strain. You shall ride with the advance forces," Colonel McDowells said decidedly, and then turned away.

CHAPTER X.

A HOT CHASE.

The two lads were well content with the assurance given by Colonel McDowells, even though each would have been forced to admit, in event of close questioning, that, while eager to bear a full share of all the dangers, the prospect of taking part in a pitched battle brought with it a certain degree of nervous apprehension.

It was known because of what Ephraim Sowers had told, and could have been well understood even though the Tory lad had not chosen to purchase safety by revealing the secrets of those whom he claimed as friends, that Major Ferguson's force was intrenched after such fashion as was possible, and, in addition, the position was rendered yet stronger by being on the mountain, up which the "rebels" must climb in order to make an attack.

Another advantage which the Britishershad, was in point of weapons and ammunition. They were thoroughly well equipped with the best quality of arms, with powder and ball in abundance, while the friends of liberty had but a scanty supply of either.

Despite such facts, however, not a man among those who had sworn to relieve the colonies from the yoke of the oppressor counted the odds. The only thought was that at last the Britishers were where a battle could not be avoided, and the mountain men were determined that the conflict should result in a victory for the "rebels."

The troop did not begin the march as soon as Colonel McDowells had proposed, however.

Although the colonists were few in numbers and with scanty outfit, there was much to be done by way of preparation for the unequal struggle, and when an hour had elapsed they were yet in camp, but nearly ready to set out.

During such time Nathan and Evan had nothing to do save watch the movements of those around them, without being able to take any part in the work, and although both were in need of repose, it was impossible to rest at a time when they were laboring under the mental excitement caused by the knowledge of what was before them.

Now and then one or another of the men would question the lads regarding their reconnoissance of Major Ferguson's camp, when Ephraim Sowers was captured, and in the course of such conversations the two boys soon learned where their prisoner had been taken.

One of the squad which had been charged with conveying the young Tory beyond reach of those who would have hanged him without loss of time, returned to camp in order to accompany his comrades on the march which it was believed would be ended by a battle, and displayed no little curiosity as to how Ephraim had been captured.

"To hear the young villain talk, one would think a dozen men couldn't overpower him. He declared that his reluctance to shed the blood of former playmates saved you lads from death."

"It would seem that he has recovered somewhat from his fears," Nathan replied with a hearty laugh. "When I last saw him he was playing the part of coward to perfection."

"He insists that you took advantage of his former friendship, and while calling for assistance, basely fell upon him when he was giving the aid you begged for."

To Nathan there was something extremely comical in such a story as told by Ephraim Sowers, who never displayed the slightest semblance of courage save when there was no possible chance he could come to any harm.

Evan's anger was aroused, however, and without delay he not only explained how they had captured the Tory, but gave additional details concerning the incident at Captain Dillard's house, when Ephraim suddenly found the tables turned upon him.

"He could not have attempted to do a more deadly wrong than when he gave information which he fully believed would result in the death or capture of Colonel Clark's force at Greene's Springs," Evan said in conclusion, "and while Nathan and I have given our word that he shall be held safe from personal harm, I hope careful watch will be kept upon him. Insignificant though the lad is, he may be able to do us very much injury."

"Joseph Abbott has been detailed to guard him," the trooper said thoughtfully, "and perhaps a more steady man should have been assigned to the work. Abbott means well; but is inclined to be careless, although it's certain he understands how necessary it is the Tory be held safely this night."

"Yes, and for many a long day to come," Nathan added gravely. "Until the Britishers have been driven from the Carolinas, Ephraim must be held close prisoner, because it is in his power to give them all needful information as to our probable movements. There can be no question but that his father aids in the work, and while it is not generally understood that such is the case, much harm can be done."

The trooper felt confident that Abbott could be relied upon for twenty-four hours at least, because he would remain at his own home, and surely there he should be able to make certain the prisoner did not escape.

Then the conversation turned upon the probable battle, and this was of such vital interest to the boys that, for the moment, they almost forgot such a lad as Ephraim Sowers ever had an existence.

It was fated, however, that they were to drop him from their thoughts for some time to come, and soon there was more reason than ever before to fear his power of working mischief.

Word had been passed for the horses to be saddled preparatory to beginning the march toward King's Mountain, and Nathan and Evan were attending to the steeds which had been provided for them, when a sudden commotion on the outskirts of the encampment caused every member of the troop to look about him in alarm.

The sound of voices in loud, angry conversation could be heard; but it was not possible for the lads to distinguish any words save these:

"He should have been hanged! It was little less than a crime to allow him to live!"

"Of whom are they speaking?" Evan asked in surprise.

"It can be none other than Ephraim, and yet I had supposed he would be forgotten, until after the battle."

"The men must have learned more of his doings, for certain it is that no one has given him a thought during the last half-hour."

A moment later it became evident that whatever had caused this last outburst against the Tory spy was of considerable importance, for the cries of anger were redoubled as a full third of the little army ceased their work of preparation to gather around the officers' quarters.

"Something has gone wrong!" Nathan exclaimed as the confusion increased. "When the command has been given for us to saddle, the men would not spend valuable time crying out against such as Ephraim Sowers. Can it be possible he has escaped?"

"That is an idle proposition, for Joseph Abbott could not have been so careless," Evan replied; but there was a sudden tremor of his voice which told that he was not as confident as the words implied.

The boys no longer gave any heed to their steed; but pressed on toward the throng which was surging around the officers' quarters, until it was possible to hear yet more of that which the excited men said.

"Abbott was the last man in the Carolinas who should have been trusted with such a duty!"

"If we had hanged the villain it would not now be possible for him to do us so much mischief!"

"Now that the Britishers are certain to be warned of our movements, there is little hope of taking them by surprise!"

These and similar remarks gave the eager, perturbed boys a fair idea of what had occurred; but yet Nathan would not credit that which appeared to be a fact until having more definite assurance that the young Tory was in a condition to work wrong to the patriots of the Carolinas.

"What has happened?" he asked of a man who was insisting that the officers were guilty of a great crime when they prevented the men from hanging the prisoner.

"Happened?" the man repeated angrily. "That young Tory whose neck should have been stretched an hour ago, has given Joseph Abbott the slip, an' is most likely on his way to King's Mountain in order to inform Major Ferguson of what we would have done this night!"

"Ephraim escaped?" Evan repeated in dismay, and immediately there came to him the knowledge of all it might be possible for the Tories to effect.

It was certain that once Major Ferguson had been warned of the proposed attack, it would be so guarded against that a heavy loss of life on the part of the Americans must inevitably be the result, and prudence would dictate that the movement be abandoned.

Insignificant though Ephraim Sowers was, he now had it in his power to save the king's troops from severe loss, and could, most likely, thwart the patriots at the very moment when they might strike such a blow as would free the Carolinas from the invaders.

The escape of the Tory was the most disastrous happening that could have been brought about by the enemies of the colonies, and the knowledge that it was possible only by sheer carelessness on the part of a true friend to the Cause, served to aggravate the offense which had been committed.

Here and there a man swore to hang Joseph Abbott if he dared to show himself in this section of the country again, and the more hot-headed demanded that

Colonel Campbell and Colonel McDowells should suffer in some way because of having interposed to save the prisoner's life when there were troopers standing by ready to execute him.

During ten minutes or more the tumult was great; all discipline had been lost sight of, and there seemed every danger much mischief would be done by those justly angry men who believed themselves thus prevented from breaking the rule of the king in the Carolinas at the very moment when it might have been successfully accomplished.

During this time Nathan and Evan had been forcing their way toward that point where Colonel McDowells and Colonel Campbell were facing the angry soldiers, believing for the moment that an attack was about to be made upon them, and then it was Evan's father spoke for the first time since the lads had come within earshot.

"I am ashamed that men of the Carolinas will thus cry out for the death of a boy, how ever much injury he may have done, or can yet do us. We war against the representatives of the king, not with children."

"It was he who would have compassed our death!" one of Colonel Clark's men shouted vindictively.

"Very true, and it is right that he be deprived of his liberty; but more than that would have been a stain upon your honor such as could never be rubbed out."

"If he had been held prisoner we should have remained silent," another soldier cried. "Now he is turned lose to carry Major Ferguson such information as will put to naught all our efforts."

"Is Abbott here to say how the lad escaped?" Colonel Campbell asked.

"His wife came with the news that her husband has gone on the trail of the viper."

"Then who shall say that such mischief has been done?" Colonel McDowells cried, his voice taking on a more hopeful ring. "To hear such bewailing as you men are indulging in, one would say there is no remedy left us. It is probably true the Tory has escaped; but he cannot have very much of a start, since no more than three hours are passed since he was led from this camp. There are twenty-eight miles between us and King's Mountain. We are ready to set out at once. Will you admit that such horses as are owned by you may not cover that distance before a boy can do so on foot? Shame upon you for thus showing the white feather when there is a possibility of repairing the mischief!"

Some of the throng stepped back a few paces as if regretting that they had been so loud spoken; but the greater number remained in front of the two officers in a defiant and angry attitude.

"Where is Evan McDowells?" the colonel cried, raising his voice that the question might be heard throughout the encampment, and he had no sooner spoken than Evan and Nathan forced their way through the crowd until standing directly before the officer, who added to the insubordinate men, "My son and Nathan Shelby—the same lads who captured the Tory—shall go out in search of him. Half a dozen more will be sent in as many different directions, and instead of standing here indulging in vain words, we may repair the mischief. This, however, I demand, and will consider him my personal enemy who disobeys what is a positive command: When the spy is retaken, see to it, each and every one, that his life be held sacred! These boys gave him an assurance, in return for certain information, that he should not come to harm, and I will never allow such pledge to be broken."

"We shall only be safe when he is dead!" a trooper cried in a surly tone.

"And you are willing, Angus McLeod, to admit that you are afraid of a boy!"

"Ay, Colonel McDowells, of such a boy as is that young Tory. While he lives we know full well all our doings will be carried to the king's officers."

"How may that be now that we have come to know him for what he is? A month ago it was different, because you allowed him in and around your encampment; but to-day, with full knowledge of his character, how can he do you harm? When he is taken, as I feel certain he must be within a short time, turn him over to me; I will be personally responsible that he no longer has the power to work us an injury."

Then turning from the discontented men as if he had done with them, the colonel said to Evan and Nathan:

"Lads, now has come the time when you may perform such a service for the Carolinas as, perhaps, is not within the power of any other. I do not hold that you are more skillful or keen on the trail than your companions; but there is in my mind the belief that you will succeed where older searchers may fail. Set out immediately; spare not your horses, nor yourselves, until Ephraim Sowers is once more your prisoner."

"But in event of our being so fortunate as to come upon him, sir, we shall be deprived of taking part in the battle," Evan said mournfully, and his father replied quickly, but in a whisper:

"There will be no battle if he escapes to carry information to Major Ferguson."

"There will be in case we shall make him prisoner within a few hours."

"In that event you may leave him with Abbott, whom, I dare venture to say, will not give way to carelessness again, or in the custody of any whom you know to be true. We shall ride the direct trail to King's Mountain, and you should be able to overtake us if the work be performed quickly."

There was no thought in the mind of either lad that such an order as the colonel had given could be slighted, and while it would have grieved them to the heart had an engagement come off while they were absent from the troop, neither hesitated.

As they turned to leave, Colonel Campbell gave orders to several of the men that they ride at once in pursuit of the late prisoner, and Nathan whispered to his comrade while they walked as quickly as the throng would permit toward where their horses had been left:

"I am not positive, Evan, how we might carry ourselves in the midst of a battle. While neither of us would admit to being cowardly, it is possible we showed a certain amount of fear when brought face to face with the king's troops. Now we have one more opportunity of proving ourselves equal to the part of men, without chance of displaying the white feather."

"I fail to understand the meaning of so many words," Evan replied petulantly. "To me the only thing certain is, that we may not follow where much honor is to be won."

"If it should so chance that we come upon Ephraim Sowers, when others failed of finding him, we will gain more credit than if we rode in the front ranks of those whom I hope will charge Major Ferguson's force before to-morrow night. Let us give over repining at what cannot be changed, and set ourselves about the task of running that miserable Tory down!"

Evan was not disposed to look at the matter in such a light, although never for a moment did he dream of disobeying his father's commands. To him this setting off on a blind search for the young spy was simply shutting themselves out from all chance of riding with the men of the Carolinas when they charged the enemy, and it seemed for the moment as if no greater misfortune could befall them.

However, he made no protest against whatever his comrade suggested, although confident that with a start in his favor of even one hour, it would be impossible for them to overtake Ephraim Sowers, more particularly since half a dozen men were to join in the hunt, and without loss of time the two lads made ready for the search.

There was no thought of making provisions for any lengthy absence; the work, to be of any avail, must be done before midnight, and if at that time the Tory was yet at liberty, then might the searchers return to their comrades, for it would be good proof Ephraim had succeeded in eluding them so far as to be able to give Major Ferguson information of what was afoot.

Therefore the only care was to make certain their supply of ammunition would be sufficient for a spirited attack or resistance, after which they rode through the encampment, and half a mile beyond were halted by Mrs. Abbott, who was returning slowly to her home.

"Are you young gentlemen setting out in search of the Tory?" she asked when the two lads halted in response to her signal.

"We are, and many others will ride on the same errand."

"The soldiers were so angry with Joseph that I had no opportunity to repeat all the message he sent. It was not through the fault of my husband that the prisoner escaped; he was left bound by the hands as when brought to our house, while we made ready a room in which he could be safely kept, and by some means managed to free himself."

"We have no time for such unimportant particulars," Nathan interrupted. "The main fact is that he is free, and we are among those charged with the search for him."

"Joseph set out on the same errand within five minutes after his escape was discovered, and he bade me say to whosoever might come, that the trail led over the hills to the westward. You will have no difficulty in following it, and should come up with my husband before riding very far."

"We thank you for the information, and would ride ahead if you are able to direct us to your home," Nathan replied.

Mrs. Abbott, who appeared to be in deepest distress because the prisoner intrusted to her husband's keeping had made his escape, gave the boys ample directions for finding the house and as the two rode rapidly forward Nathan said in a hopeful tone:

"There is yet a chance, Evan, that we shall succeed where the others failed, thanks to our having met Abbott's wife. If the trail is well-defined, we shall be able to ride it down, capture the spy, and return to the encampment before our people have set out.

"That is what we should do, but whether we can or not is quite another matter," Evan replied gloomily. "It is a pity we promised the Tory our protection, otherwise he would have been beyond all power for harm long ere this."

"And would you like to remember that we captured a lad who was once our friend, for others to hang in cold blood?"

"Almost anything would be better than that we were shut out from following those with whom we should ride this night."

"I am counting that we will yet bear them company," Nathan replied cheerily. "Even a Tory cannot make his way across the country without leaving a trail, and now that we know where it may be taken up, the rest ought to be easy."

"Unless he has suddenly lost his senses, we cannot follow him on horseback. If I was trying to escape from mounted men, it would not be difficult to strike such a course as should be impossible for them to follow."

"That he did not do so at the start is positive, else Abbott would never have sent such word by his wife," Nathan replied, heeding not the petulance of his comrade. "If we hold to it that Ephraim Sowers has made his escape, then is he the same as free, but I shall continue to claim we have fair chance of overtaking him, until we know beyond a peradventure that he cannot be found. Every second is of value to us now, and we'll waste no more time in idle talk."

With this remark, which Evan might well have construed as a rebuke, Nathan struck his horse sharply with the spurs, and the two quickly left Mrs. Abbott far in the rear.

CHAPTER XI.

SUCCESS.

In silence the two lads rode on at the full speed of their horses until they were come to the home of the man who had caused so much trouble through his carelessness, and here Nathan dismounted, leading his steed by the bridle as he made a complete circuit of the building.

To boys who had been taught the art of woodcraft because it was absolutely necessary they should be expert in following a trail or hiding one, it was a simple matter to ascertain where the Tory had made his escape from the house, and at what point he struck into the woods, although a person ignorant of such matters might have looked in vain for any token of the flight.

"There's no need of spending much time over such a plain sign as that," Evan said, now recovered somewhat from his petulance, for hope that they might soon recapture the spy had sprung up in his heart. "I never would have believed Ephraim Sowers was such a simple as to thus give information regarding his movements! Surely he knew Abbott would set out at once in pursuit, and yet has made no attempt to hide his trail."

"He is a coward who allows his fears to blind him from anything except immediate danger. Having seen an unexpected opportunity to escape, he takes advantage of it, and thinks only of putting a great distance between himself and his enemies. We shall soon ride him down!"

"Unless he gathers his wits, and takes to the thicket where we cannot follow."

"Then it will be necessary to make our way on foot, and I'll warrant that we travel as fast as he can. But I'm not allowing he'll gather his wits until having come to a British camp."

During this brief conversation Nathan remounted, and the two rode along the trail, having no difficulty in keeping well in view the signs left by both the pursued and the pursuer.

Abbot had taken good care not to cover the footsteps of the Tory, and to leave ample token of the course he was following; therefore it was certain the lads must soon come upon one or the other, since they were well mounted.

There was one danger Evan had failed to realize, but which was strong in Nathan's mind. If Ephraim could retain his liberty until night came, then would it be well-nigh impossible to follow him during the hours of darkness; and this very important fact may have been in the spy's mind when he pushed on regardless of thus giving good proof as to his whereabouts to those who might come in pursuit.

Therefore it was Nathan rode on at the best speed of his horse, and his comrade found it difficult to maintain the pace, consequently there was no opportunity for conversation during twenty minutes or more, at the end of which time they were come up with Abbott.

That the trooper was suffering keenest mental distress because of his carelessness, which had permitted of the spy's escape, could readily be seen even during the hurried interview they held with the man.

"You are come in good time, for the Tory can't be more than a mile ahead of us," he said with a sigh of relief. "The sun will not set for two hours, and long before then you should have him in your keeping once more."

"You will follow as close as may be, for we count on turning him over to you again in order that we may ride to King's Mountain with the American force," Nathan replied, not averse to giving his horse a brief breathing spell.

"You may be certain he won't get out of my sight again! Any other might have had the same misfortune as I. His hands were bound, and I left him in an upper room while I made ready the chamber that was to serve as prison."

"Why did you not keep him with you?" Evan asked sharply.

"That is what should have been done, as I now know full well; but at the time it seemed as if the lad was as secure as if surrounded by a troop of soldiers. Certain it is he can't free his hands, and, therefore, must necessarily travel slowly. I suppose every man at the camp bears down heavily upon me?"

Nathan would have evaded this question; but Evan was minded that the careless soldier should be made to realize how great was his offence, therefore he answered bluntly:

"I believe of a verity you would have been hanged had it been possible for the men to get hold of you when the news of the escape was first brought in. If Ephraim Sowers succeeds in remaining at liberty, the attack upon King's Mountain will be abandoned, and that at a time when it might have been a success but for your carelessness."

"See here, Abbott," Nathan added soothingly, "it is not for me to deny the truth of what Evan says; but he is describing that first moment of disappointment. Your comrades have grown more calm by this time, and if it so be we overhaul the Tory, it is Colonel McDowell's orders that he be given into your custody again."

"I'll shoot the villain rather than let him get a dozen yards from me, if he falls into my clutches once more, an' I've sworn not to go home inside of forty-eight hours without him."

It was in Evan's mind to say that it would have been better had Abbott kept a close watch of his prisoner, in which case such desperate measures would not now be necessary; but he realized in time to check his speech, that harsh words were of no avail now the mischief was done, and contented himself with the caution:

"It will be well to remember how much trouble has been caused, if we are so fortunate as to catch the Tory. My fear is that he may succeed in giving us the slip after all, in which case the attack on Major Ferguson's force is frustrated even before being made."

The horses had been allowed as long a resting spell as Nathan thought necessary, and he brought the interview to an end by saying as he tightened rein:

"We shall ride the trail at our best pace, and do you follow on until finding that we are forced to leave the steeds, when it will be known that there is no longer a hope of taking him in time to set the fears of our people at rest before the hour for making an advance. In event of our coming upon him, we shall be glad to turn him over to your keeping once more, as soon as may be possible."

"I'll keep mighty near your horses' heels, unless you ride at a better gait than I believe will be possible. Don't hesitate to shoot him down if you get within range and find there's a chance of his getting the best of the chase."

"There's no need to give us such advice," Evan replied grimly. "Do your part at holding him, if it so be you have another chance."

Nathan had urged his steed forward, and the two spurred on at a sharp trot, each rider's eyes fastened upon the ground where could be plainly seen, by those accustomed to such work, the footprints of the Tory.

Evan was rapidly recovering from the fit of petulance which had seized upon when it appeared most likely they would be shut out from riding into battle with the American force.

Now it began to seem possible they might perform the task set them and return to the encampment before the advance was begun, unless it so chanced that Ephraim Sowers suddenly showed sufficient wit to seek refuge in a thicket where the horses could not follow.

Something of this kind Evan said to his comrade as they rode on the trail nearly side by side, and the latter replied cheerily:

"The miserable Tory don't dare do anything of the kind lest he lose his way. I venture to say his only thought is that Abbott will set out in pursuit of him, rather than spend time by going to the encampment, therefore he has only to fear what one man afoot may be able to do. It hasn't come into his thick head that the woman could be sent with a message, while her husband took to the trail, therefore he will hold to the open path until hearing the hoof-beats of our horses."

And this was indeed what Ephraim Sowers did, as his pursuers soon learned.

Nathan and Evan rode swiftly and in silence during twenty minutes or more after leaving Abbott, understanding full well that the trail was growing fresher each instant; and then the former saw a certain suspicious movement of branches at one side of the path some distance away.

"He has seen us!" the lad cried excitedly, spurring his horse forward until he came to that point where the trail suddenly branched off toward the thicket.

There could be no question but that the Tory had failed of hearing the noise of the pursuit until his enemies were close upon him, and then he did what he should have done an hour before.

There was not a second to be lost, for once the lad was so far in advance that his movements could not be followed by the motion of the foliage, it would be like the proverbial hunt for a needle in a haystack to find him.

"Look after the horses!" Nathan cried, reining in his steed and leaping to the ground musket in hand, and even before Evan could come up, although but a few paces in the rear, Isaac Shelby's nephew had disappeared in the thicket.

Young McDowells was not disposed to obey this command strictly. He cared for the steeds by hurriedly tying their bridles to the trunk of a tree, and after a delay of no more than half a minute, followed his comrade into the forest, with musket in hand ready to be discharged at the first glimpse of the fugitive.

So close behind Nathan was Evan, that he could readily follow his movements by the commotion among the underbrush, and, with a sudden burst of speed, regardless of possible accident, he succeeded in coming close to his comrade's heels.

"Have you lost sight of him?" he asked breathlessly.

"Not a bit of it!" was the cheery reply. "There is little fear he can give us the slip now we are so near!"

"Why don't you fire on the chance of winging him? I can give you my loaded musket when yours is empty."

"There's no need of wasting a cartridge upon him; we shall soon bring the villain in sight."

It was not possible to carry on any extended conversation while running at full speed among the foliage, at great risk of falling headlong over a projecting root, or being stricken down by a low-hanging limb.

They were gaining in the chase as could readily be seen, and when perhaps ten minutes had passed the lads were so near that it seemed certain Ephraim could be no more than a dozen yards in advance.

"No one can say what accident may happen at any moment to give him an advantage!" Evan said sharply, speaking with difficulty because of his heavy breathing. "You must bring him down soon, or we may get back to the encampment too late!"

No suggestion could have been made which would have had greater weight than this; and, raising his voice, at the same time priming the musket as he ran, Nathan cried:

"Come to a halt, Ephraim Sowers, or I shall fire! At this short range there is little danger but that my bullet will strike its target, with such good token of your whereabouts as you are giving us."

The Tory made no reply; and the waving of the bushes could still be seen, thus showing that he had not obeyed the command.

"Do not delay, but shoot at once, and then exchange muskets with me!" Evan cried in an agony of apprehension, lest some unforeseen chance give the fugitive such an advantage as they could not overcome.

Nathan hesitated no longer. Raising the weapon he fired in a line with the moving foliage, and the report of the musket was followed by a scream as of pain.

"I'm sorry I didn't wait a few minutes longer!" the lad cried, in a tone of deepest regret. "Of course we were bound to stop him; but it might have been done without killing!"

Evan shared his comrade's regrets, believing Ephraim had been seriously if not dangerously wounded, and the two ran forward with all speed, fully expecting to find their enemy disabled or dead.

Therefore was their surprise all the greater when the swaying of the branches told that the Tory was yet able to keep his feet, and once more Nathan shouted, this time in a tone of anger:

"Halt, or I shall fire again! Give me your musket, Evan, and do you load this one! Work quickly, for I'm not minded to linger over the task of stopping him!"

The exchange of weapons was made without delay, and once more Nathan fired. Again came a scream as of pain from the fugitive; but this time the pursuers were not troubled in mind lest they had needlessly inflicted pain.

Nathan leaped forward as he discharged the musket, and an instant later stood face to face with Ephraim Sowers, who, with a rotten branch upraised as a club, stood at bay where a perfect network of trees, that had most likely been overturned by the wind, barred his further passage.

"I'll beat your brains out!" Ephraim screamed viciously, brandishing his poor apology for a weapon. "Don't make the mistake of thinkin' I'll be carried back among them rebels!"

"You had better give in peaceably, for we shan't spend much time in arguing the matter," Nathan said decidedly; but yet he did not advance for the very good reason that he was virtually unarmed, having dropped his musket at the moment of emptying it, in order that he might not be impeded in his movements.

Because he remained motionless, Ephraim believed the lad was afraid, and pressed his supposed advantage by crying, in a tone that was very like the snarl of a cat:

"Keep your distance or I'll kill you! This club will stand me as good a turn as the empty muskets do you, an' I count on using it!"

By this time Evan came into view carrying both weapons, and, seeing that the game was brought to bay without opportunity of continuing the flight, said quietly:

"Keep your eye on him, Nathan, and I'll soon put in a charge that will bring him to terms."

He had begun to load the musket as he spoke, doing so with deliberation as if there was no good reason why he should make haste; and such leisurely movements had even more effect upon the Tory than did the show of ammunition.

"I didn't count you had more than a single charge," he said, with a whine.

"It seemed odd to me that you should suddenly have plucked up so much courage," Nathan replied scornfully. "Even though our ammunition had been exhausted, you could not have held us back with that rotten club. Load carefully, Evan, for I don't want to make any mistake as to aim!"

"Are you countin' on killin' me?" Ephraim cried, in an agony of terror, flinging down his poor weapon and holding out both hands in supplication. "Would you murder a fellow who never did you any harm?"

"You are the veriest coward in the Carolinas;" and Nathan spoke in a tone of such contempt that even the thick-skinned Tory winced.

"Come out here, and we'll make certain of taking you back to Broad River!"

The Tory meekly obeyed, making no show of protest lest he might bring down the anger of his captors upon himself; and Evan said, as he finished loading both weapons:

"Do you walk ahead, Nathan, and let him follow. I'll come close at his heels, and we'll spend no more time over this job than may be necessary. Abbott should be near at hand by the time we get back to the trail."

Ephraim obeyed in silence and, because he neither begged nor whined, the boys feared lest he had some plan of escape in his mind.

"Do not take your eyes from him for a single instant," Nathan cried warningly as he led the way in the manner suggested by Evan, "and shoot at the first suspicious move he makes. We have done this work in short order, and now it will be because of our own carelessness if the troop sets off without us."

"Don't think that I'm going to be so foolish as to make another try at gettin' away," Ephraim said sulkily. "There's no show for me in this section of the country while the king's troops are so far away, an' I ain'tcountin' on takin' the chances of bein' shot."

"We shan't be so foolish as to take your word for it," Evan replied. "I'll admit that you won't make much of a fist toward escaping; but time is precious with us just now, and we can't afford to waste any in chasing you."

From that moment until they were come to the trail where the horses had been left, no word was spoken; and then the lads were greeted by a cry of joy and triumph from Abbott, who had just come into view.

"I knew you'd overhaul him!" the trooper said exultantly; "and if he gives me the slip again there'll be good reason for my bein' hanged!"

"Do you think it will be safe for us to leave him here with you?" Nathan asked, as if undecided what course he ought to pursue.

"I'll answer for him with my life! Don't think there is any chance of slipping up on the work again, after all that's been in my mind since he got away."

After a brief consultation the two lads concluded it would be safe to leave the prisoner with Abbott, particularly since Colonel McDowells had so instructed them; and in less than two hours from the time of leaving the encampment, they were riding back at full speed, hoping it might be possible to arrive before the force had started on the march toward King's Mountain.

And in this they were successful.

The soldiers were on the point of setting out when the lads arrived, and the reception with which they were met can well be imagined.

As soon as their story could be told, and it was generally understood there was no longer any reason to fear that Ephraim Sowers might carry information of their movements to Major Ferguson, the command was in motion, with Nathan and Evan riding either side of Colonel McDowells.

In the report of the battle, which is signed by Colonel Benjamin Cleaveland, Colonel Isaac Shelby, and Colonel William Campbell, is the following account:

"We began our march with nine hundred of the best men about eight o'clock the same evening, and, marching all night, came up with the enemy about three o'clock P.M. of the seventh, who lay encamped on the top of King's Mountain, twelve miles north of the Cherokee Ford, in the confidence that they could not be forced from so advantageous a post. Previous to the attack, on our march, the following disposition was made: Colonel Shelby's regiment formed a column in the center, on the left; Colonel Campbell's regiment another on the right, with part of Colonel Cleaveland's regiment, headed in front by Major Joseph Winston; and Colonel Sevier's formed a large column on the right wing. The other part of Colonel Cleaveland's regiment, headed by Colonel Cleaveland himself, and Colonel Williams' regiment, composed the left wing. In this order we advanced, and got within a quarter of a mile of the enemy before we were discovered."

Evan and Nathan rode by the side of the latter's uncle, and as Colonel Shelby's and Colonel Cleaveland's regiments began the attack, they were the first in action.

"I am growing timorous," Evan whispered to Nathan as the troops began the ascent of the hill, and the latter replied:

"A fellow who spends twenty-four hours in walking, and twenty-four hours in riding, without repose, can well be forgiven for losing some portion of his courage. My own knees are not oversteady, and I am beginning to wonder whether they will bear me out when we are within range of British lead."

Five minutes later Major Ferguson's force opened fire, and Colonel Isaac Shelby had no cause to complain of the lads' behavior.

As Evan afterward admitted, he was hardly conscious of what he did from the moment he saw the first man fall.

One of the troopers reported to Colonel McDowells, who asked concerning his son after the engagement was at an end:

"The two boys fought side by side, and like veteran soldiers. I saw them making their way up the hill when the shot was flying around them like hail, and it was as if neither realized the peril, or, realizing it, as if he heeded not the possibility that death might come at any instant. Never faltering, they continued the ascent, pressing close on Isaac Shelby's heels until they were the foremost, fighting hand to hand with the Britishers.

"They were within a dozen feet of Colonel Williams when he received his death wound, and then the redcoats were pressing us so hotly that no man dared step aside to aid the officer. Yet these two went out of their course to give him succor, and, finding that he was already unconscious, pressed forward once more. I was just behind them when we arrived at the spot where Major Ferguson lay dead."

"Evan feared his courage might fail him when in the heat of action," the colonel said half to himself, and the trooper replied with emphasis:

"It must have increased rather than failed, colonel, for those two lads shamed many a man of us during the hour and five minutes which we spent grappling with the Britishers. Twice were we forced to fall back; but they remained in the front line, and each time when we rallied they were first to take the forward step. Not until Colonel Depuyster hoisted the white flag did I see them cease their efforts, and then, the excitement being gone, it was as if both of them collapsed, and little wonder, colonel, for if you will stop to think, these lads spent forty-eight hours riding and walking before going into as hot an engagement as we in the Carolinas have ever experienced."

The battle of King's Mountain came to an end as the trooper had said, in one hour and five minutes after it began, and when the American forces were drawn up in line it was found that of the nine hundred, only twenty were killed; but more than five times that number had been wounded.

Of the king's soldiers, four officers and fifteen privates were killed, and thirty-five privates seriously wounded. Eighteen officers and fifteen privates were taken prisoners. Of the Tories, five officers and two hundred and one men were killed; one officer and one hundred and twenty-seven men wounded, while forty-eight officers and six hundred men were taken prisoners.

According to the official report of that engagement, only twenty of Major Ferguson's force escaped, and among that number, one—Ephraim Sowers—could be accounted for as already a prisoner in the hands of the Americans.

The historian, Lossing, writes regarding this engagement:

"No battle during the war was more obstinately contested than this; for the Americans were greatly exasperated by the cruelty of the Tories, and to the latter it was a question of life or death. It was with difficulty that the Americans, remembering Tarleton's cruelty at Buford's defeat, could be restrained from slaughter, even after quarter was asked.

"On the morning after the battle a court-martial was held, and several of the Tory prisoners were found guilty of murder and other high crimes and hanged. Colonel Cleaveland had previously declared that if certain persons, who were the chief marauders, and who had forfeited their lives, should fall into his hands, he would hang them. Ten of these men were suspended upon a tulip tree, which is yet standing—a venerable giant of the forest. This was the closing scene of the battle on King's Mountain, an event which completely crushed the spirits of the Loyalists, and weakened, beyond recovery, the royal power in the Carolinas. Intelligence of the defeat of Ferguson destroyed all Cornwallis' hopes of Tory aid. He instantly left Charlotte, retrograded, and established his camp at Winnsborough, in Fairfield District, between the Wateree and Broad Rivers."

It was because of Sarah Dillard's ride that the battle of King's Mountain became possible, and consequently it was through her indirectly that the royal power in the Carolinas was "weakened beyond recovery."

In telling the story of her brave act, it has been necessary to introduce the two lads who bore so honorable a part in that brief campaign, and also the Tory spy, but it is not possible within the limits of this tale to follow the adventures of the two young Americans who, before the independence of the United States was gained, made for themselves most enviable records among most gallant men.

At some time in the future, when the reader shall be ready to go into the more important engagements with Evan and Nathan, a further account of their deeds will be set down, and then can be described all which Ephraim Sowers finally did to clear his name of the taint which had been put upon it by his own deeds.

It suffices now to say that the spy was held as prisoner by Colonel McDowells for two months or more, when, agreeably to his sworn promise that he would never do aught against the cause of freedom, he was released with the understanding that he should leave the Carolinas forever.

Within one week after the battle of King's Mountain Nathan and Evan were regularly enrolled among the soldiers under Colonel Charles McDowells' command, and when General Cornwallis surrendered were among the troops who had contributed to that officer's discomfiture.

It was on the day set for the formal surrender at Yorktown when the two lads were standing side by side in the ranks, that Evan whispered to his comrade:

"Who ever dreamed on that night when Ephraim Sowers lorded it over us at Captain Dillard's home that we should stand here waiting to see the proudest general among all the Britishers give up his sword to the 'rebel' commander?"

"Do you know that this victory was really begun when Sarah Dillard rode over the mountain trail to Greene's Spring, for from that moment all General Cornwallis' power in the South began to wane."

THE END